S0-BNT-070

For the pooches
In memory of Watson and Minnie
And for Zig, slobber and all

ACKNOWLEDGMENTS

To:
Richard Jackson, for being such a gent about tarot.
Susan Burke, whose generosity and enthusiasm
got me through some tough times.
Russell Gordon, Greg Stadnyk, and Jessica Sonkin,
who created so many gorgeous covers.
Liselotte Watkins, for her lovely illustrations.
Amy Berkower, for working so hard to get this series right.
Emma Dryden, for her patience and sense of humor.
Jeannie Ng and Alison Velea, who are just great.
Paul Crichton, for giving this series so much time and energy.
Cindy B. Nixon, for her thoughtful, sensitive work.

DEATH.

KNIGHT of WANDS.

II

XI

QUEEN of PENTACLES.

I never wanted to do a reading. I hate those cards. Maybe they do tell the future, but so what? Who wants to know the future?

I know Eve—and Anna, though she'd never say it—thinks I'm the world's biggest chicken. I don't mind admitting it. The world is scary. People are cruel. I know we're supposed to think everyone's nice at heart and if you just get to know them, you'll see they're really good inside. But if you've seen what people can do to animals, you'd know there are some seriously unnice people out there.

I guess what I mean is, I'm not the kind of person who jumps into things. I'm not Eve, who has no problem waving a hand in the world's face and yelling, Hey, look at me!

Like this musical she did. If they'd asked me to replace the star at the last minute, I'd have thrown up. Or fainted. Or both. Which would have been quite pretty.

I'm not like Anna, either. Anna thinks we're more alike in that neither of us is super confident. But Anna does so many brave things without knowing they're brave. She doesn't think twice about taking care of her little brother. She doesn't think it takes courage to get dumped by a boy you're crazy about and not fall apart. But I saw what she went through, and I know different.

In fact, after the Declan Disaster, I told Anna I wished I were braver. She said, "You're crazy. Who saved Mrs. Rosemont's cats?" She was talking about these cats her neighbor left behind when she died. She gave one to Anna, but the other two went to people who didn't really want pets. Animals like that can end up abandoned, so I found the cats new homes. It wasn't that hard. One's with Eve, and I have the other, Beesley, who's the sweetest thing ever.

I said, "Yeah, but that's easy."

Anna raised her eyebrow, but for me, it is easy. If it's a choice between calling a total stranger and knowing I left some poor thing with an owner who didn't want it, well, that's an easy choice.

"And you played the piano for Eve's show," said Anna. "That took huge guts."

I smiled, because it's true that at first I was nervous about *playing in front of people. But when I play, it's like the real world disappears. All I think about is the music. So that's easy too.*

But talk to kids I don't know at school? Forget it. Raise my hand in class unless I'm absolutely one hundred percent certain of the answer? No way. Approach an actual male-type person and say, Would you like to hang out sometime? *Yeah, right. Just thinking about it makes my stomach lurch.*

Maybe that's just how I am. Hey, the world needs chickens, too, right? But sometimes I worry that I'm going to go through my whole life doing the same old things year after year. New people, new places—my brain starts churning out "What ifs": What if something goes wrong? What if they think I'm an idiot? What if I wreck everything?

It drives my mother bats. When I tell her I don't want to go to school dances or compete in some music contest, she clicks her tongue and says, "Syd-ney." And I know she's thinking, How'd I end up with such a coward for a daughter?

She's always on me to make new friends. I'm like, "I have friends. I have the best friends in the world." She once said, "You have to get out there, honey. It doesn't make you disloyal to Anna and Eve to have other friends. Someday the three of you won't be so joined at the hip. People change, new things come along. What will you do when that happens?" All I could think was, I don't know. I hope it never does.

The one person who truly gets me is my dad. He never

pushes me to "get out there." And when my mom does, he says, "Leave her alone." Like when this teacher at Anna and Eve's private school heard me play and pushed me to try for Julliard, my mom was thrilled. My dad had to say for me, "Forget it. That place is too pressured for Sydney." And he should know, he went there.

(The one thing I don't like about my dad standing up for me is that I hate being another thing he and my mom fight about. They fight enough as it is. My mom's friend Liz says some people just like screaming—which I don't get at all.)

It was my dad who showed me that if you're a chicken, music can save you. He showed me how music creates a whole other world, without people and all their drama. When I was six, he took my finger and pressed one of the low keys.

"What does that sound like?"

"Sad," I said. "Scary. But . . . ," I guessed, "nice, too. Like I want to hear it again."

"That's the thing about music," he told me. "It takes pain and turns it into something beautiful."

When my dad was young, everyone thought he would be a world-famous musician. We have a scrapbook full of pictures of him playing in concert halls, winning competitions. But the pictures stop when my dad's around twenty. He didn't become a world-famous musician. He became a teacher instead.

Once I asked him if he minded not being a famous

musician. He said, "Wasn't good enough." He didn't say if he minded or not.

But more and more, I think he does. 'Cause it's not only my mom he fights with. Two years ago he lost his job because he screamed at the principal. He got a new job, though, and basically, everything's been fine.

But last night, when I got home from the cast party for Eve's show, I could feel it: Something had happened. Something really bad.

Which is why, even though I hate the cards, I called Anna this morning and told her I wanted to do a reading.

ONE

When dealing with a frightened animal, it is essential to establish trust. Approach slowly, giving them plenty of room. That way, you minimize the risk of flight or aggressive reaction.
—*Carr's Book of Animal Care*

"Oh, my God, are you okay?" Anna grips the door, staring at me with huge eyes. Guess I sounded pretty upset on the phone.

Well, Anna, either my life is falling apart or I'm freaking out over nothing. This is why I need those stupid cards.

But before I can say anything, the apartment buzzer rings. Anna says, "There's Eve. I called her and said to come over," and goes to buzz her in. As she does, I imagine their conversation: *Syd's having a nervous breakdown! Get over here now!*

A minute later Eve comes tearing out of the elevator, shouting, "Guess what? Guess what? Guess WHAT??"

She charges through the door and into the kitchen, where Anna has breakfast laid out. Tearing a pumpernickel bagel in half, she says, "No, don't guess. I mean, you can if you want, but you'll never get it." She slathers cream cheese on the bagel, stuffs it in her mouth.

I say, "Eve, you're scaring me."

Around a mouthful of bagel, Eve yelps, "My reading was right! It was right, right, right!" She jumps up and down, slamming her feet into the floor.

"How, how, how?" cries Anna.

"Guess who called me this morning? Hint: Starts with a 'P.'"

Anna gasps. "Peter McElroy?"

"Mr. *You Suck!* himself." Eve grins. "Guess what he wanted?"

I say, "He's putting you on his TV show . . ."

Anna chimes in, "He wants to sign you to a record contract . . ."

"Well, he wants me to try out for his show," says Eve, slightly deflated. "His new one about talented kids. *Making It!*" Then, regaining her psycho energy, she squeals, "Amazing or what?"

"Abso*lute*ly amazing," declares Anna.

"Not so amazing," I say. "You're insanely talented—and you were nice to his daughter. He owes you."

"But that's not why he's doing it," says Eve triumphantly. "He thinks I'm good, he thinks I'm good, he thinks I'm good." She flops into a chair. "Soon I shall escape from my heinous parents and my lo-o-ser brother, Mark." Eve hates her older brother, who could not be more different from her. If there's such a thing as anti-siblings, Eve and Mark are it.

"When's the audition?" Anna asks.

"In two months. In Philadelphia. You guys *have* to come. I must have my entourage."

"We'll be the goofy friends who wait outside and cheer when you make it," says Anna excitedly.

"Whoo-hoo! Road trip!" says Eve, punching the air. "Well, with my mom, but we could probably ditch her without too much trouble."

"You are so mean to your mom," says Anna.

"Oh, you're not mean enough to yours." She sits ups. "Right, so that's my fabulous life sorted out. What *I* want to know"—she waggles her eyebrows at Anna—"is what happened with Nelson last night."

Anna goes very red and gets deeply involved with

9

spreading cream cheese on her bagel.

Nelson is a boy at Anna and Eve's school, who—according to Eve—has liked Anna for eons. Only, Anna was with this guy Declan, and Nelson was too shy to butt in. But since she and Declan are history, and she and Nelson were making out after the party last night, I'd say he got over his shyness.

"So . . ." Eve settles her arms on the table. "How does he kiss?"

Anna pelts Eve with a bread pill. "None of your business."

"Oooh, that bad?"

"No—that good." Eve laughs. Realizing she's been tricked, Anna throws another bread pill at her.

But then she turns serious, saying, "Now, wait a minute, Miss Syd. We're here to talk about you. What's going on? You sounded totally freaked on the phone."

Eve swings her gaze to me. "Syd time!"

I bite into my bagel and chew so I don't have to answer right away. Anna and Eve are so happy and excited; they're worlds away from everything I'm feeling. I feel embarrassed, like I've done something weird and if I tell them, they'll say, *Oh, we understand.* But, really, they'll be shocked. Like, *God, can you believe what's going on with Syd?*

I'm not used to talking about myself. I've always

been the listener, the one who gives advice. Maybe that's boring. But it's better than having people stare at you, waiting for you to spill your ugly secrets.

And not just my secrets, but my dad's.

I shake my head. "You know what? I made too big a thing of it."

Anna says, "So, tell us what it is, so we can agree with you."

Tell us. Sounds simple. So why do I feel so scared?

Well, guys, when I got home from the party last night, I found my mom sitting in the kitchen, clutching a mug of tea. I said, "Where's Dad?"

And she said, "You know, that's a very good question."

Then my mom got up and went to my dad's study. Knocking on the door, she said, "Syd's home, Ted. Do you think you can come out now?"

Which was fairly bizarre. And it got even more bizarre when my dad said, "Not now, Miranda."

So what does my mom do then? She says, "You're not keeping any secrets here, Ted."

I was like, Secrets? What is going on?

My mom went on. "Marty called me from school. I know what happened."

And then my dad said, "Good for you. Now you know."

So you're probably wondering what happened, what the big secret was. Well, here it is. On Friday my dad threw a chair

11

across the classroom. There weren't any students around, but other teachers saw it. And they reported it. And now the school is deciding if my dad gets to keep his job.

And that's not even the worst part.

Later that night, when everyone was supposed to be asleep, I heard someone walk down the hall to the kitchen. I waited a few minutes, then got out of bed and followed.

My dad was standing in the dark. There was a glass on the counter and a bottle of expensive booze someone gave my parents at Christmas. My dad screwed the cap off, poured some into the glass.

I said, "Dad?"

My dad didn't look up. Just put his hands on the edge of the counter and gripped it like it was the only thing holding him up. He said, "Go away, Sydney."

I really didn't want to leave him like that, so I said, "I could just—"

But he didn't let me finish. He slammed his hand on the counter, shouted, "Now, Sydney!"

My dad has never hit me. But now I know what it would feel like if he did.

I remember saying "Okay" or something dumb like that. Then, as I was about to leave, I heard my dad say, "Syd—I'm sorry."

I don't know if your parents have ever apologized to you. You'd think it'd be great, right? Hey, finally, they admit *they're wrong about something. But this didn't feel great. It felt frightening. Like my dad didn't know what he was doing any more than I did, and if I was scared for him, he was ten times as scared.*

So, ever since then, guys, I've been all about "What ifs." What if my dad does lose his job? What if he can't get another? What if my mom gets so pissed off, she leaves him? What if . . . ?

I can feel Anna and Eve staring at me, and it's like someone's put a sweaty hand on my face and won't let me breathe.

"Guys, I freaked out over nothing. It's . . . we don't have to talk about this."

"But we can if you want to," says Eve. I know she's trying to be a good friend. But Eve loves drama, particularly anything about screwed-up parents, because her parents drive her nuts. If I tell her what's going on, she could say it's a deep, dark, awful thing just because she likes deep, dark, awful things.

"Yeah, but I don't want to," I say as lightly as possible.

"You sounded so upset on the phone," says Anna.

"I was tired from the party. Really, guys, I'm serious. I don't want to talk about it." My voice rises. Trying to sound normal, I say, "You know me, I'm a big chicken."

I concentrate on picking out another bagel. As I do, I can feel Anna and Eve looking at each other, trying to decide, *Should we push her?*

Eve will say *Yes, push* with her eyebrows. Anna will say *No* with a little shake of her head.

And I guess Anna wins, because the next thing I hear is her saying, "God, can you believe it's almost summer?"

Grateful for the switch in subject, I add, "Freedom, just four weeks away!"

"*Finals,* just three weeks away," says Anna.

Eve sits back, grinning. "Ah, you poor suckers, worrying about finals. For some of us, that's all a distant, painful memory."

"You'd better worry about finals," says Anna sharply. "You could still get kicked out."

"Who cares? Once I get on *Making It!,* I'm out of there anyway."

"What if you *don't* get on *Making It!*?" I say.

"There is zero chance that will happen," says Eve, sticking her finger in the cream cheese and licking it off. "Remember my reading? Fame, fortune, all that good stuff? The audition is just the next step toward my ultimate destiny. School? Forget it."

"Wait, you'd leave me alone in that horror hole?" Anna says.

"Hmm," says Eve, pretending to think about it. "School versus megastardom—tough choice. Anyway, what do you care? You're going to be busy with your 'love.'"

Anna blushes. It's true that when she was dating Declan, she did get a little obsessed; and, yes, it did get annoying. But Nelson is very different. I'm sure it won't be the same—at least, I hope.

"So—what?" says Anna. "You're not even a star yet and you're ditching us?"

Eve heaves a weary sigh like we are mere children and she must explain the ways of the world to us. "All I'm saying is, maybe we have to face the fact that it's time to pursue our own destinies. You and Nelson, me and certain fame, Syd and . . . whatever your destiny is." She frowns at me. "I wish you'd do a reading so we could find out."

"Forget it," I say instantly. "No way."

"You should know what's coming," Eve argues. "Be prepared."

Right, I think. *I should know that my dad is falling apart, that my parents are splitting up, that . . .*

"Sorry," I say. "My future will just have to remain a mystery."

Eve scoops up the last of the cream cheese with her finger. For a moment I think she's going to keep pushing, but she says, "Whatever. I gotta hit the bath-room."

While she's gone, Anna says, "Do you think she's serious about blowing off finals?"

I hesitate. "I think she's just excited, talking big. But maybe we should study together, help her focus."

"Excellent." Anna smiles. Then, tracing the pattern on the tablecloth with her finger, she says, "I know you don't want to talk about it. But if . . ."—she struggles, not sure how to put it—". . . if you get scared over noth-ing again, will you call me?"

I don't know what I'm more grateful for: that Anna cares or that she's pretending to believe I got scared over nothing. "Yes."

"Promise?"

"I promise."

Anna has to take her little brother, Russell, over to a friend's, so it's time for me and Eve to leave. I live in the same building, but I go with Eve to the lobby. In the elevator she talks about her audition. She's so jazzed, I don't really get a word in. Just a lot of "Hmms" and "Yeahs."

But then, all of a sudden, she breaks off her *Making It!* monologue. "You're cool, right? Like, if there was something really weird going on, you'd tell me?"

Startled, I give her the same answer I gave Anna. "Yes."

"Because if you're not happy, I want to know about it. 'Cause that's just wrong."

She's so fierce, I give her a hug. "I am totally fine, I swear." Eve glares, like she's checking for signs that I'm lying. I do my best to look fine.

As I watch Eve put on her headphones, I think of how she loves people so hard, even though she pretends she doesn't. And how Anna always tries to be sensitive to what you want, even if she thinks you should do just the opposite. With friends like that, how could I be anything but totally fine?

So . . . why don't I feel happier?

It's time to pursue our own destinies. You and Nelson, me and certain fame, Syd and . . . whatever your destiny is.

Even though we're different, I've always thought of me, Eve, and Anna as equals. Eve is the crazy one, Anna is the together one, and I'm . . . well, I don't know what I am. The crazy-about-animals one. The never-fights-with-anyone one. When Anna and Eve argue, I act as the peacemaker. I like that—being a little on the outside, not getting too caught up in whatever.

But now I really feel on the outside. And not in a good way.

Someday the three of you won't be so joined at the hip.

People change, new things come along. What will you do when that happens?

Why do I feel like someday is here and I am not prepared?

When I get to my door, I hear music. My dad's playing our piano. Turning the key, I have a memory of being little, falling asleep on the couch while my dad played, then being lifted up and carried to bed. I'd be a little awake but pretend to be asleep so he wouldn't put me down.

The first piece he ever taught me was "Heart and Soul." He started me off on the easy part, the *duh, duh, duh, duh,* while he did the melody. Then he let me work my way through the melody. I remember seeing my hands next to his on the keys, thinking they'd never be as big as his, never reach as far.

What if the school called? What if my dad's been fired? What if he and my mom are waiting for me? *Sydney, your dad and I aren't going to be living together anymore. . . .*

I take a deep breath and open the door.

Beesley comes padding stiffly down the hall to welcome me. He probably spent the morning in my room, following the sun patch around the rug. Beesley loves sun.

The first time I met him, he was hiding in a box in a stranger's apartment. I whispered to him, and he stared at me with those enormous gray eyes, like, *That's okay, I know nobody cares about an old cat like me. I'll just stay here, not bother anyone.*

And that's Beese. He's such a gent. He never wants to be a nuisance or put you out. Anything you give him, he's so grateful for.

I know he doesn't have a lot of time. His kidneys aren't in great shape, and he needs special food and medication twice a day. On rainy days he walks stiffly, so he must have arthritis. He can't leap onto my bed like my last cat, Widget, could. You have to lift him up and help him down. He's light, like he's made out of balsa wood. I always tell him, "You're so easy to carry."

My parents were not thrilled when I brought him home. My mom sighed and said, "I see vet bills in my future."

Which was seriously cold. Like, I couldn't believe how cold. I said, "Well, I could just take him to the vet right now. Say, 'Here, he's old, get rid of him.' I mean, if he's going to be such a pain and so expensive . . ."

My mom shook her head. "That's not what I'm saying, Sydney."

"I can pay for it," I blurted out. "Whatever the bills are, I'll pay. I have money. I just don't think you should give up on someone just 'cause they're a little old and sick."

That's when my dad got up and put his arm around me. "Nope. Nope, nope, nope." He kept saying it like a magic word. He kissed me on top of the head. "You're right," he said into my hair. "You don't give up because someone's a little creaky in the joints."

I pick Beesley up, because it's time for his medication. As I do, I see my dad standing in the hallway. He's a big guy, a little tough-looking. Everyone says I look like my mom, and I guess I do, but I always think that's weird when I *feel* so much more like my dad.

Only, after last night he feels like a stranger. Like the one you're not supposed to open the door to, even if they seem okay.

His hands wander in the air with no place to go. He says, "Hi."

I say "Hi" back.

I'm terrified I'm going to get another "Sorry." I don't want sorry. I don't want to talk about last night at all. It's too ugly, too weird. I step back with Beesley in my arms.

My dad notices. His shoulders slump. Now I feel rotten.

I say, "I need to give Beese his meds." Like this explains why I'm backing into the kitchen.

Relieved, my dad asks, "Mind if I observe the healing touch in action?"

"Nope."

We go into the kitchen, and I get Beese's drops down from the cabinet. You have to squirt the drops into the back of his mouth. This means holding his mouth open gently, so you don't hurt him. As I massage his jaws, I glance over at my dad, who's standing at the counter. That's exactly where he was standing last night. Only then it was dark, not the middle of the day, with sun streaming through the window. And he was hanging on to the edge as if he were about to fall—not leaning against it and smiling.

Reality is so weird. One moment, it can be one thing, the next moment, the total opposite.

I make gentle noises to Beese as I squirt in the medicine, stroke his head as he gulps it down. My dad says, "Hey, Beesley—you know you landed with a girl in a million, right?"

"He's a cat in a billion." I pet Beesley to make him forget the meds, then set him down. He walks out of the room. Slowly, as if he doesn't want to be rude. But he likes to be alone after he has his medicine. I think it's a pride thing.

I glance at the cabinet where my parents keep stuff

like the salad bowl and cutting boards. And alcohol. I wonder if that bottle is still in there.

I take a deep breath. "Did the school call?"

"Tomorrow," he says. "They don't fire people on Sundays." He drums his fingers on the counter as if he's playing it. "I gather your mom told you."

"She said you threw a chair. But that it didn't hit anybody."

"Yeah." He smiles slightly. "I missed."

I try not to smile back. "Dad, it's not funny."

"No, you're absolutely right." He says this with a straight face, but I admit, I immediately think of this group of girls at my school who have decided that they're vastly superior to everyone else and that this gives them the right to be cruel to anyone weak enough not to fight back. I imagine throwing a chair at them, watching them fall like bowling pins.

"What do you think'll happen?" I ask.

"They'll fire me," he says simply. "Or they won't."

I want to say I hope they don't. But it feels like something my mother would say, which feels wrong.

My dad asks, "Where were you off to this morning?"

Oh, I was going to find out if you were having a nervous breakdown. "Breakfast. Anna and Eve."

My dad nods. "And how are Anna and Eve?"

"Good." I hesitate. "Anna has a new boyfriend. Oh, and Eve has this big audition for a TV show."

"Well, that's earth-shattering." My dad hates TV.

I smack his arm. "It's pretty cool, come on."

"I can think of cooler things."

"Yeah, like what?"

"Oh . . ." My dad frowns up at the ceiling like he's giving this serious thought. "People who stick up for the lost souls of this world, for one. Girls with red hair, for another. The two together . . ."

I smile. "Yeah, okay. I get it." And I do.

This is my dad knowing I feel left behind and trying to make me feel better.

This is my dad saying he's sorry he told me to go away.

This is my dad.

TWO

Many animals find strength in the pack or pod or herd. United with their fellows, certain of their status within the group, they have a sense of security. Separated from them, they may feel anxious, even desperate.

—*Carr's Book of Animal Care*

"Hey, Syd."

"Hi, Syd."

"See you tomorrow, Sydney."

As I walk down the hall to my locker, I think about how, for most people, "hi's" and "hey's" are not a big deal. Amazingly, most people are able to say hi or hey or have a nice whatever back without even thinking about it. To them, these things do not feel like a test they haven't studied for and will absolutely fail.

But every time someone says hello to me, I feel a tiny burst of panic. Is there something they expect me to say? What if I don't say it? What if they're nicer to me than I am to them? What if they think I'm stuck-up? And because I always freeze, people probably do think I'm stuck-up. My "hi's" totally suck. They're little whispered things you can barely hear. I once tried a "How are you?" and nearly gagged.

A girl from my German class walks by, says, "Hey, Syd, how are you?"

I go, "Hi," and keep walking. Then, at the stairs, I realize I never answered her question. Like, how hard would "Fine" have been? Or "Good"? Or "Okay"? Or any one of the million things normal people know how to say?

Four weeks left till summer. In four weeks I won't have to do this every day.

However, Anna and I have only three weeks to get Eve together for her finals. At first I thought Anna was crazy, thinking Eve would really ditch her finals because she's so convinced she's going to be famous. But when Eve asked me if she should get a white limousine or something more stylish—"like purple"—I realized Anna wasn't the crazy one. So today we're meeting at Eve's house for a power study session.

Just before I leave school, I go to the bathroom and brush my hair. Then I get out my one tube of lip gloss and put some on. Finally, I stare into the mirror and think, *Who are you kidding?*

This is my normal ritual before I go to Eve's house. Why? For the dumbest reason in the world. It's the same dumb reason I'm wearing my plaid miniskirt instead of jeans. The same reason I washed my hair last night. It's not a reason I would ever tell Eve—or even Anna. Because if she found out, Eve would kill me. Or die laughing.

I am pathetically in love with her brother, Mark.

And I think Mark knows it.

A few months ago, as I was leaving Eve's house, he got in the elevator at the same time as me. At first I cringed in the corner, thinking, *Say nothing. Don't speak. Because what if . . .*

But then I thought, *Sydney, for once in your life, take a chance. SAY SOMETHING!*

Wrong decision. What was my big pickup line? I get nauseous every time I think of it: "So, Eve says you're really into computers."

Mark stared at me. Like, *Oh, no. It spoke.*

And did Syd the Idiot stop there? No, she didn't. Syd the Idiot went on and on about how cool it was to like computers because, well, she uses one, obviously, but she doesn't have the first clue how they work. But she bets Mark has the first clue, and that's cool, because most people don't and . . .

Needless to say, Mark ran out of the elevator the second we hit the lobby.

Afterward, I thought, *Okay, this could be good. Because if I have any shred of dignity left, I will no longer like Mark Baylor. No crush can survive such humiliating rejection.*

But it turns out, I have no dignity. I'm still wearing my nicest skirt, still putting on that bit of lipstick, still hoping I run into Mark every time I go to Eve's house. I can't help it. Mark Baylor is exactly what I think a boy should be. He's incredibly smart, with dark hair and dark eyes. Yes, he wears glasses, but that means he's not snotty about his looks, which I love. He doesn't care about any of the typical "guy" things, like sports or tormenting people, the same way I don't care about typical girl things, like dumb TV or . . . tormenting people. He's tall. He's perfect. For me, anyway.

Of course, Eve thinks he's a total squid. She's always calling him "M.A.N.," which is her code for "Major Anal Nerd." Part of it is that Mark does everything right in their parents' eyes, and Eve . . . well, "right" isn't her thing. She pretends not to care, but of course she's jealous. So telling her that I, too, like Mark is completely out of the question.

Not that it matters. Mark Baylor is never going to be into me. Since the elevator disaster, he makes a point of disappearing whenever I'm around.

But as I ring the doorbell, I can't help thinking that nature wouldn't make you like someone so much if there was no hope of them ever liking you back. Someone so perfect for you has to see one day that you are perfect for him. And that—

The door opens, and there before me is Mark. Looking terrified.

Wanting him to understand that I am not stalking him, I say, "I'm here to see Eve?"

He opens the door an inch, says warily, "She's not here."

This is a first. Mark has never actually spoken to me before. Despite the fact that it's obviously torture for him to do so, I am thrilled. Then I realize I don't understand what he said.

"What?"

"Eve—she's not home from school yet."

"Really? We're supposed to study together." *No, Syd, no! Mark does not care what you are supposed to do. Please, have a little pride!*

"Ah, well, that explains why she's late," he says. "In fact, it would explain if we never see her again." He steps away from the door. "You can wait for her if you want."

As I walk through the door, I'm thinking that, for any other girl, this would be an opportunity. A chance to overcome that catastrophe of a conversation. Anna could do it. So could Eve. But Syd the Idiot, who can barely say hi to people at school—forget it. *I should have been a cat,* I think. *Cats never have to say hi to people. Or a goldfish. Or a . . . slug. A tiny, slimy, insignificant slug.*

I say, "I'll just wait in the . . ."

I'm talking to no one. Mark has vanished. Sighing, I decide to wait in the kitchen. It's the farthest room from his, and hopefully, he'll see that I'm trying not to be a pest.

But when I go into the kitchen, I find Mark at the refrigerator with the most adorable look of disgust on his face.

I step back. "Oh, sorry."

He looks over the open fridge door. "For what?"

I gibber, "Well, this is your kitchen, and I'm barging in . . ."

"You're not a barger." He frowns into the fridge. "You don't even qualify as a barger-in-training."

29

He opens the refrigerator door wide. "How many science experiments would you say are taking place in this one fridge at this moment?"

I peek. There does seem to be a large number of take-out containers with dark and mysterious things growing inside them. Half-finished yogurts with the foil partway on. Some wrinkly vegetables in the bottom drawer. The milk is not from this week. Actually, not even from this month.

"You guys eat out a lot," I say as he shuts the door.

"My parents aren't fully domesticated beings." He blinks at me. *Now what do I do with it?* "You want a glass of water or something?"

I swallow. "Sure."

He picks a glass out of the dishwasher, fills it with water, and hands it to me. "I don't think this will kill you."

I nod my thank-you. Clearly, Mark's decided that even if I do have a crush on him, I am too sad to do anything about it and therefore safe.

"Well," he says, "got to . . ." He points down the hall.

"Right," I say. "Thanks for the water."

"There's more of it. In the tap. If you want."

"Great." Mark looks at me like, *That was a joke, dummy.*

I sit down at the kitchen table and sip the water. On a heinous scale of 1 to 10, that Mark encounter was about a 6—really not that bad. I didn't impress him. But I don't think I humiliated myself. Some level of dignity was maintained.

I take another sip, look at my watch. Anna and Eve are half an hour late. Late is normal for Eve—but Anna? Maybe they got held up at some school thing.

To pass the time, I imagine the perfect girl for Mark. She is dark and intense-looking. Beautiful, wears glasses, and is able to talk about all the things he cares about, especially computers. She's not a shy, redheaded giraffe. I hate her.

Another five minutes pass. Torn between annoyed and worried, I get out my cell phone to call Anna when I hear a yowl from the hallway. All of a sudden, Mark lurches into the kitchen. Followed by Tatiana, Eve's white Persian.

Mark scrambles onto the sink. "It was in my room. I don't know how, but it was in my room."

Tat yawns, pretending to be unaware of the drama she's caused. Of Mrs. Rosemont's three cats, Tat is the most beautiful and the most arrogant. As I pet her, she blinks up at me like, *Gently, handmaiden, gently!*

Mark says, "I don't suppose I could pay you to lock her in the bathroom."

"Are you allergic?"

"No," he says, his eyes never leaving Tat. "Just . . . averse."

Okay, reason number 347 Mark Baylor will never be into me. He hates cats. Chances that he will fall for a cat-loving gal—nil.

Picking Tat up, I say, "She won't hurt you, I promise."

He nods. "Okay, you've promised. Now make her go away."

"How can you not like . . ." I'm about to say "cats," but that seems harsh. ". . . Tat? Look how beautiful she is."

"She's a snot," he says.

I turn Tat toward me, stare into her green eyes. "Well, if I looked like her, I'd be a snot too."

"Ech," says Mark. "She's not so hot. If she were a girl, she'd be one of those blond 'Aren't I so gorgeous? Don't you worship me?' types. Besides . . ."

I look up from Tat. "What?"

"Never mind." He shifts on the sink ledge. "So, what—you're some fearless lion tamer? No animal too fierce? Cats, dogs, crocodiles . . ."

No animal, I think, *just humans.* "Crocodiles might be a little much."

Which is a joke—not a good joke, maybe even a

bad joke, but so much better than the usual mess that comes out of my mouth around Mark that I smile at him.

At which point I see from the clock on the wall that it's been an hour since Eberly let out. This is late even by Eve's standards. In fact, this is no longer late, this is—

Mark notices me looking at the clock. "Eve blew you off," he says matter-of-factly.

Now Mark knows that, not only does he not want to be with me, but even my supposed best friends have better things to do. Embarrassed, I say, "I probably had the wrong day." As I say this, I think Mark's fantasy girl-friend would never get the wrong day. Mark's fantasy girlfriend is so fabulous, she keeps other people waiting. They don't even mind, that's how fabulous she is.

"I should go," I say, getting up.

"Oh." Mark squirms on the sink. "Do me a favor? Before you leave?"

"What?" A flare of hope that he will say, *Don't leave, be with me, giraffe girl* . . .

He points to Tat. "Put that in Eve's room."

On the way home I tell myself that obviously, I got the wrong day. Eve might blow me off—but Anna? Not possible. Idiot Syd screwed up.

Only, when I get to my room, I see the Post-it where I scribbled *Power study Monday!* And I know I didn't screw up.

They blew me off.

Which feels a hundred times worse.

Maybe something awful happened. Something at school and they had to stay late. A something so big, they forgot to call. Or maybe . . .

Maybe that's just the way things are going to be from now on. Eve is famous, Anna's in love. Syd is nowhere.

Or what if . . . the school blew up? Or they were hit by a bus?

Or captured by aliens. Sydney, cut it out.

Opening my e-mail, I sit down and type, *Hey, guys. Was I totally crazy, or were we getting together today? Probably, I'm just insane. Ignore the crazy girl!*

Then I wait. Five minutes . . . ten . . . twenty . . .

Half an hour later a message from Anna pops up: *OH, MY GOD, SORRY!!!! Can't believe I forgot. What a loser! Chorus practice . . .*

Twenty minutes later a message from Eve. *Chorus practice? Please. Somebody needed goo-goo time with her boyfriend.*

Not sure Eve meant to hit Reply All on that one.

A minute later a message from Anna. *Actually,*

somebody *had to brag to Mr. Courtney about her* Making It! *audition—again.*

Then from Eve: *Actually, somebody was talking to Mr. Courtney. But they were mostly talking about Syd! Syd, Courtney still thinks you should do that Julliard thing. What can I say, the man's a maniac.*

I smile. Mr. Courtney did the musical at Eve and Anna's school. I played at rehearsals, so he could direct. He's very nice but very crazy. He kept telling me I was good enough to go to Julliard. But I'm pretty sure he was being kind because I was playing for free.

Anna writes, *Syd, were you stuck outside waiting?*

I type: *No, Mark was home. We hung out in the kitchen.* I don't know why I have to share that, maybe to say, *I wasn't alone, just waiting for you guys!*

From Eve: *Mark? Now I really do feel bad. Poor you!! Disinfectant a MUST!*

From Anna: *Yes, beware nerd cooties.*

I grit my teeth, wanting to write back in all caps, *Well, he was there, you guys weren't, so shut up!*

But instead I type: *So, when's the next study session? Tomorrow after school?*

For a little while, nothing. Then Anna: *Tomorrow's not so good for me.*

Date with Nelson, I think. I write: *That's cool. Eve, you want to hang?*

Eve writes back: *Oog. My dad and I are going to check out this voice teacher.*

I take my hands off the keyboard. Take a deep breath, then type: *Whenever everyone wants to get together, I'm good.*

I wait for the message that says, *Yeah, definitely.* Or, *How about the day after tomorrow?* It doesn't come.

For a while I sit, trying to decide what's going on. Is this a calamity that marks the beginning of a pitiful, friendless life or just one not so great day?

Then I hear the front door slam, my mom and dad coming down the hallway. My mom is saying, "I just think you have to . . ." and my dad answers, "Okay, Miranda, *okay.*"

Oh, God, the school. They were deciding today. I bet my dad's been fired. And, of course, my mom is lecturing my dad to do this and do that. She's always giving advice just when you feel at your most rotten and don't want it.

I go out to the hall. My parents are standing by the door to their room. My mom is rubbing her forehead. My dad has his arms folded. It feels like there's a cement wall between them.

I say, "What happened?"

My dad looks up, sees my face. "Oh, honey . . ."

He comes over and hugs me. Into his shirt, I ask, "Did they fire you?"

He laughs a little. "No, no, they didn't. In fact, there's good news. For a change. Guess who's the new instructor for Erikson's Summer Music Study Program for Gifted Students?"

I put my finger on his arm, and he nods. "Really?"

"Really." I give him a hug. He hugs me back, and I feel how happy he is to be wanted. I guess the school finally realized it was asking a lot of my dad to teach kids who don't care about music. So now they're giving him something he can really get into. My dad's a great teacher—with the right students.

Then he says to my mom, "Hey, let's do something crazy and celebrate."

I say, "Yeah!"

My mom frowns. "I'm having dinner with Liz. Remember?" She gives my dad a look as if he never remembers anything about her life.

I don't want my parents fighting again, so I say, "We can all go." My mom looks unsure. "Please, Mom?" I widen my eyes, trying to get across how important it is that we show my dad we're here for him. My mom is allergic to screwups; weakness is not her thing. But if she can't be happy for my dad now . . .

My dad sweeps his hand through the air. "Dinner at Chez Wong. On me, the big earner."

Mom hesitates. "I just don't want . . ."

"Oh, want anything, Miranda. Today's a good day. Let's want everything."

Mom throws up her hands. "Chez Wong it is."

Liz coming is actually perfect. She's my mom's oldest friend, and I feel guilty saying this, but I like her more than my mom. She's a vet, which is what I want to be more than anything in the world. And she has this great way of making things seem not so serious. Like when my mom moans about something her boss said or complains that my dad is rude, Liz teases her, saying, "Yes, Miranda, let's drive ourselves crazy over what the world thinks about us."

As we walk to the restaurant, I think how ridiculous I was to get so upset that night. Not one of my "What ifs" came true. My dad still has a job, my parents are still together. (Although they're not actually *walking* together right now. My dad is walking with me, my mom is three feet ahead, like she's on her own.)

My dad says, "Have you thought about your summer piece yet?"

Every summer, while my piano teacher's on vacation, my dad teaches me a new piece of music. Maybe for some kids, this would be a boring way to spend the summer, but I love it. I say, "I was thinking Schumann's Kinderszenen?"

This is a piece my dad played for me when I was little because he said it was written about childhood. It's a quiet, simple piece that feels like visiting a place you haven't been to since you were a baby. Then you come back and nothing looks as big and impressive as it used to.

"Nice choice," says my dad. "Schumann it is."

Smiling up at him, I think, *Maybe my friends did blow me off today. Maybe I don't have a boyfriend, and maybe I never will. Maybe only cats will ever hear me perform. But I have a life. A good life. I am not—yet—pitiful. And I don't need any stupid cards to tell me otherwise.*

We meet Liz on the corner outside Chez Wong. Liz is small; I've been taller than her since I was eleven. Seeing me, she says, "This girl is so tall and so gorgeous, I can't stand it. Give me a hug—maybe some of the tall, gorgeous thing'll rub off."

As we go inside, Liz pats my dad on the arm. "Congratulations, Ted. Nice news about the summer."

"Yes," says my mom. "Bullet dodged. Or should I say chair?"

Liz smiles like this is a normal joke. But my dad's jaw tenses. Sitting down, he waves the waiter over and asks for a beer. My mom says, "Ted." He acts like he doesn't hear her.

My dad's beer comes and he drinks half of it in one gulp. Liz tells a funny story about a slobbery bloodhound that came to her clinic, but Dad stares at the menu, ignoring the conversation.

Liz is imitating the bloodhound when he interrupts. "One thing that drives me crazy about this place? They don't have salt and pepper squid."

My mom rolls her eyes. "Gee, Ted. That's a blow." Clearly, she's mad at my dad for wrecking her dinner with Liz.

Liz stops telling the bloodhound story and opens her menu. I do the same, even though I always have broccoli with garlic sauce. When the waiter takes our order, Liz kids me. "Wait, don't tell me, it's . . . broccoli with garlic sauce."

"It's what she likes," snaps my dad. "Can't she have what she likes?"

Desperately wanting everyone to get along, I say, "I don't . . ."

Liz squeezes my hand, says, "Of course she can."

My mom and Liz order beers, which means they all have one! Hopefully, things can now be normal. Raising my water glass, I say, "Hey, to Dad."

"To Ted," says Liz.

My mom adds, "To success. May this work out." She sips her beer, not looking at anyone. She probably almost believes she meant that to be nice—almost.

My dad drains his beer and orders another. My mom says "Ted" again. But softly, like she knows he won't listen, so what's the point?

Liz turns to me and says, "And what are your summer plans, young lady?"

I'm about to tell Liz about the Schumann when my mom says, "Oh, hanging around the house. And . . . hanging around the house."

See, this is my mom. I do a million things in summer. Practice, study with my dad, read animal books. She calls it "hanging around."

Now she says, "What about this guy who told you about the summer program at Julliard?" I groan inside. I can't believe I was stupid enough to tell my mother that.

Even Liz looks intrigued. "That sounds promising."

My dad puts his beer bottle down. "Give me a break, that place isn't for Sydney."

"Why not?" says Liz.

"Yeah, Ted?" says my mother. "Why not?"

Now they're ganging up on him. Which is totally obnoxious. My dad knows what he's saying. He went to Julliard really young—and dropped out his second year. He says he wanted to find somewhere people were making real music, without thinking about money or fame.

I say hastily, "Because it's not. It's super competitive. I'm sure all the kids are geniuses. I wouldn't go there in a million years."

My dad smiles at me, rubs my hand. Then he orders another beer.

By the time I get my broccoli, my dad is halfway through his third beer. I think of making a joke about it. But I can't think of any way to make this funny.

As we start eating, Liz says, "So tell me about this program, Ted. Sounds great. Gifted kids, right up your alley. Considering you have one"—she smiles at me—"and you were one."

When Liz says this, I remember a picture we have of my dad as a baby. He's sitting at a piano. Someone's put his little hands on the keys, and he's looking up at whoever's taking the picture. It's a sweet picture, but it always makes me feel sad for some reason. He looks frightened, like, *Can I get down now?*

Now he shrugs and says, "What gifted kids need most is to be away from people who tell them they're gifted. Away from a school that treats them like cash cows."

"Well, you can protect them from some of that." Liz has this smile on her face that looks like it's stuck on with Krazy Glue.

I say, "Yeah."

But my dad doesn't answer. He's not eating. The only thing he takes off the table is the stupid beer bottle. After a while Liz turns to my mom and says, "How did your talk with—"

My dad breaks in, saying, "I mean, you don't think this place actually cares about music, do you? If it cared, do you think I'd be throwing chairs around?"

After a long, ugly pause my mom says, "Nobody knows why you throw chairs, Ted."

"Oh, no? Well, I'll explain it, then." He smiles at me, but it's a smile that's hiding something. Screaming or . . . vomit. "I threw the chair because the head of the school—you know, the one who cares so much about gifted kids—told me, 'Music looks good on the college resume, Ted. Nobody cares whether or not these kids are the next Itzhak Perlman.' And I said, 'Well, I don't care about college resumes.'"

"Which was incredibly intelligent," says my mom sarcastically.

Glancing at me, Liz says, "Okay, guys, let's lower the temperature."

But my dad barrels on. "It'd be one thing if the

kids cared. But they don't. None of these kids care about anything. Other than their credit cards and their clothes and . . ." His fist closes around the bottle. "They're all little consumer drones."

My mom slams down her chopsticks. "For *once*, Ted, could we not have the 'Every Child Is Evil' speech? I mean, just for a change of pace?"

I can't breathe. I'm sending ESP signals to my parents: *Stop this. Stop this now. Please stop this.*

My dad shouts, "You don't know, you're not there!"

"I might as well be," my mom shouts back. "I never stop hearing about it!"

People are turning, staring. Liz whispers, "Hey, could we—?"

"No, Liz, we could not," says my dad. And throwing his napkin on the floor, he gets up and walks out of the restaurant.

For a moment my mom just sits there, fists in her lap. I don't know why she had to start this. Tonight was supposed to be about making Dad feel good, not tearing him down. All night she was needling him, about the beer, about Julliard, even about the gifted program.

I get out of my chair. My mom says, "Where are you going?"

"Someone should be with him."

Mom rolls her eyes. "Honey, believe me, the best thing now is if your dad is left alone."

"The best thing for who?" I ask.

My mom holds her hands up, like another word and she'll lose it. I'm about to yell, *Oh, yeah, you'll lose it. Nobody feels any pain in this family except you,* when Liz says, "Miranda, check outside. Maybe he's getting some fresh air." She takes my hand, says gently, "You, sit."

My mom slaps her hands on the table. "Right. Looking for Ted. Another round of looking for Ted."

With my mom gone, there's no one but me to say to Liz, "I'm sorry."

"Sweetie, why are you apologizing?"

"Um . . . because this has been so *much* fun?"

She smiles, but the smile's a little broken. "Your dad had too much and your parents had a fight. These are not things you have to apologize for."

I nod, wanting to ask Liz what she means by "too much." Does she mean the beer? Too much anger? Too much work? It's true, now that I think of it. When my dad gets this way, it's like he's had too much of everything. Work, life. Us.

My mom comes back to the table. "Well, he's not out there."

I say, "I think we should go."

She points to my plate. "You haven't finished—"

"No, I really think we should go." I need to be out of here now. I need to be home and see that my dad is home and that while this was bad, it's not . . .

I'll just feel better when I see Dad is home.

We pay the bill. My mom smiles at the waiter, says the food was wonderful. I feel like yelling, *This doesn't matter, let's go!*

When we're outside, Liz says to my mom, "Call me." She gives me a big hug. "You call me too."

My mom and I take a cab home. As we open the door, I can feel the house is empty. My dad's not here. Beesley peeks around the corner, like, *Oh, good, you're here. I worried everyone had gone.* I pick him up and he purrs, like he knows I need to feel useful to someone right now.

I go into the living room. My mom is sitting on the couch, looking like she wants to run out the door and never come back.

I say, "You want me to wait with you?"

"No, you go to bed. This'll be dealt with by morning." Then she gets up and kisses me. But only because she knows she has to.

That night I wait for the sound of the key in the lock, watch the clock as it gets later and later. I think,

What if this is the last night we're a family? What if Dad never comes home? What if . . . something so awful I can't even think the words has happened? What if all we get is a phone call?

A little after midnight the key turns in the lock, and my dad is back. My mom murmurs, my dad murmurs back. They're not fighting. This isn't "It."

Or . . . maybe it is. Or maybe it's about to be. I don't know.

I don't know—the phrase keeps going in my head. I don't know if my parents are staying together. If my dad is all right. If Anna and Eve are going to stay my friends. . . .

I know nothing. Even about the most important things in my life. And that's because I am a chicken, too scared to look at the truth. Some lion tamer.

Then I think of the cards. Supposedly, they show you the truth, whether you like it or not. I remember Eve saying, *You should know what's coming. Be prepared.*

I don't want to know.

But . . . isn't that why I should?

THREE
SHE WHO WOULD THE FUTURE KNOW . . .

The next day I leave a message for Anna, telling her I need to see her and Eve as soon as possible. I have a speech planned if she says she can't do it or Eve's busy or whatever. But thank God, I don't have to make it because Anna calls me back right when she gets home that night and says, "Absolutely. My place after school tomorrow."

Sitting on Anna's rug, I tell her and Eve everything. How my dad threw a chair, how I found him in the kitchen drinking in the dark, and how he stormed out of the restaurant Monday night and didn't come home until after midnight.

Neither of them says a word while I talk. As I finish,

I brace myself. Now they'll tell me how awful it sounds, how sick my dad must be, how this is so much worse than anything they've ever heard.

But they don't. Anna finger fences with Mouli's tail as it twitches. Eve pulls at a loose thread on Anna's beanbag. Neither will look at me. I can't tell: Are they shocked? Or do they think I'm an idiot?

Finally, I say, "So?"

Anna looks at Eve. Eve looks at Anna. Eve says, "You know, sometimes I freak out and maybe it seems intense to other people? But it doesn't mean I'm falling apart."

"Yeah, but . . ." Frustrated, I realize that one of the reasons they're not taking this seriously is that I've never told them about my dad before. I never told them why he lost his job a few years ago. I haven't told them about how he and my mom seem to say more mean things to each other than nice things. And as long as you don't tell people things, they can think everything is okay.

Correction: As long as I didn't tell people things, *I* could think everything was okay.

Only—maybe they are? Maybe everyone's families are like this and I just think my parents are crazier than most? I ask Anna, "How did—?" Then I stop.

"How did what?" says Anna gently.

I say in a rush, "How did you know when your parents were going to get divorced?"

"Oh." Anna thinks a moment, then says casually, "Well, the nonstop fighting was kind of a clue."

"How nonstop? Like, every day or . . . ?" Because my parents don't fight every day. At least I don't think they do.

Anna draws her hand down Mouli's stripy back. "I remember sometimes thinking, 'Oh, my God, this is it. They are definitely getting divorced.' Then nothing would happen. One time they got really ugly with each other, and I yelled at them, 'Why don't you just split up?' And they were, like, shocked. 'We're not getting divorced! What makes you think we're getting divorced?' Then a year later, 'Uh, by the way, we're getting divorced.'"

"So they lied."

"Maybe?" Anna shrugs helplessly. "But also to themselves, if that makes any sense."

Okay, so no answers there. What else? Remembering the way my dad drank those beers, I ask, "Do your parents drink?"

Eve grins. "You should see my dad at weddings. King of the hora."

Anna says, "My mom has wine with dinner."

"Does she get weird?"

Confused, Anna shakes her head. Eve explains to her, "Like, does your mom get silly?"

"No," says Anna. "Oh, yeah, once? She went out with some friends and she came home a little giggly. Like, all of a sudden, *everything* was fine. She was fine, I was fine, the world was fine." She smiles at the memory. "She was a wee bit tipsy."

Silly, giggling. This is not my dad.

This isn't getting me anywhere. Taking a deep breath, I say, "I want to do a reading." Anna immediately shakes her head. "Why not?"

"Just . . ."—she squirms—"this is serious, you know?"

"You asked about serious things." I look at Eve. "You asked whether your career would work out."

Eve says, "Yeah, but this is your dad. This is . . ."

"Real life," I finish for her.

"Yeah, kind of." She looks sheepish. Here she is, always bugging me to do a reading. Now she's trying to talk me out of it.

Mouli pads over to me. I stroke his ears. Mouli is a big orange thug. He doesn't always like to be petted. But today he seems to know I need something to hug—although he's also sort of pretending it's not happening, that he's still a tough guy.

I say, "If it's real life, doesn't that make it more important to know the truth?"

"But the cards . . ." Anna hesitates. "You don't always know what they're saying."

"They came true for you, right? And for Eve?"

"But not the way we expected," says Anna. "At least me."

"I don't care what happens in between," I say. "As long as they tell me my dad's going to be okay, that's all I care about."

Eve leans forward. "Yeah, but what if . . . ?" She can't finish the sentence.

"Then I should know, right? The cards show one version of the future, right? And you can change it if you make changes in the present."

"But you have to make the right changes," says Anna. She looks at Eve. "I didn't, did you?"

Eve frowns. "It's weird. When you get caught up in fate, you kind of lose track of what's the right thing to do and what you're destined to do. Are they the same thing or not? Sometimes I did lousy things because I thought it would get me closer to my 'fate.'"

I look down at the rug. That's where Anna always lays out the cards. Nothing there now but shadows.

I can't leave here without doing a reading. I can't walk away from something that might tell me the truth.

I say the words. "I want to do it."

Anna peers at me. "You're *sure*?"

"Yes."

Anna takes a deep breath and goes to get the cards. I look at Eve. What I see in her face scares me. She looks nervous, and Eve is never nervous.

Then she says, "What are you going to ask?"

I hadn't actually thought about it, putting everything I'm feeling into one little question. Images of my parents screaming come into my head. My dad throwing a chair, walking away from us. *I'm sorry.*

Out loud, I say, "I guess, is my dad going to be okay?"

"Well, you know he totally will be," says Eve.

"Yeah." For the first time, I smile. "But I'll feel better knowing." Listening to Anna rummage around in her closet, I ask, "You think the cards really work?"

Eve grins. "Hey, look at me."

True. They promised Eve the World, which is everything good you could possibly hope for. Her whole life has changed since she did her reading.

Will my life change? Do I want it to?

Anna comes back with the cards, sets them down in the middle of the rug. It occurs to me: We always sit in a circle when we do this. Which is appropriate, I guess. There's supposed to be something powerful about circles. And threes—there are three of us. *And three cats,* I think, looking at Mouli, who's sitting between me and Anna. Maybe it's my imagination, but I swear, he's staring at the floor, waiting for the cards to go down.

I reach for the box, look to Anna for instruction. She says, "Shuffle the cards while you think about your problem. Don't talk, just . . . think."

"Okay." I take the cards out of the box. They feel stiff and awkward in my hand, like a stranger who gets annoyed when you ask directions.

"They're hard to shuffle," I say as I start.

"Shh," says Eve. "Let your mind wander."

I wish she and Anna weren't treating this like it's some solemn ritual. It makes me nervous that if I don't think the exact right things or shuffle the cards the exact right way, I might get some terrible prophecy of doom.

Dad, I think, breaking the cards apart. *Think about Dad.*

So I do. I think about that beer bottle at dinner, about how angry he got when he was talking about his job. I remember *Go away* and my mom talking through the closed door.

"Don't only do bad stuff," Anna whispers. "Think about the nice things, too."

I nod, feeling the cards loosen under my fingers. I think about how my dad let me keep Beesley, how he closes his eyes when he plays the piano, how it's nice to be the daughter of someone who's that great, to have even a little tiny bit of that talent. . . .

Then I think, *Why are you doing this? Why are you telling everyone your dad has problems? So he gets angry. So he drinks. People do much worse stuff every day. He's a great guy, a million times more interesting than most dads.*

Then, for no good reason, I find my mind wandering to Mark.

I hesitate. "When do I stop?"

"When you're ready," says Eve.

I set the cards down. "I'm ready . . . I guess."

"Ask your question," Eve reminds me.

"Oh, right." I swallow, squeeze the cards tight. "Uh, is my dad going to be okay?"

"Now turn over the first card," says Anna.

My hands are shaking. "I don't know how. Can you do it?"

Taking the deck from me, Anna lays out the cards. The first one is a man looking at a bunch of cups. Each cup has something in it. One has jewels, another has a snake. Did I get cups because of my dad's drinking?

I ask, "Is that good or bad?"

"Let's see," says Eve, picking up the book that

tells what each card means. "The first card shows you where you are now, whatever craziness you're going through." She frowns at the book. "Hmm. The Seven of Cups. 'Fantasy, daydreams, wishful thinking.'"

"So maybe I did overreact," I say hopefully. "Maybe it's a worrywart fantasy, and my dad's fine."

"Yeah, but wishful thinking? You wouldn't *wish* to think he's sick," argues Eve.

"Let's look at all the cards," says Anna, taking the book from Eve. I'm glad; Anna's more sensitive. "Next card"—she points to the one laid sideways over the Seven of Cups—"this is about an opposite force, something that's helping or fighting you in this situation. Like a clash that's causing the tension." I nod, thinking "clash" is the right word because the card shows a picture of a sword.

"Ace of Swords," says Anna. "'Determination, love, force, success.'" This sounds much better than some dippy daydreamer, and I perk up. "Or," says Anna, "because it's sideways and we're not sure if it's upside down or not . . . 'violent temper, disaster, self-destruction.'" She rubs my shoulder. "Sorry."

"That sounds a little like my dad," I say, my throat tight. "They both do. So—what are the cards saying?" Which is more powerful? Love or destruction?

"We don't know," says Eve. "What's the next one?"

She points to the card below the first two. "This is your distant past."

"The Two of Pentacles," says Anna. "Not sure how this works. 'Difficulty. Inability to launch. Embarrassment.'" She looks at me. "Does that make any sense to you?"

Embarrassment? Absolutely. Inability to launch? I think of myself at school, the way I can't speak to anyone, feel like a sputtering, useless rocket that struggles up only to topple over. Since I've felt that way my whole life, this makes sense for my distant past.

Then, for some reason, I have a flash of the picture of my dad as a kid at the piano, all that meant-to-be stuff that never was. But that's my dad's childhood. Why would it turn up in my reading?

Bored with the distant past, Eve says, "Next."

"Recent past, Nine of Swords," says Anna, pointing to a card that shows a woman in bed with a bunch of swords hanging over her.

Anna hesitates. "Well, okay, this is no surprise. 'Concern, anxiety over a loved one.'"

I feel a chill. I knew the cards got some things right, but I've never been sure how much Anna and Eve were reading into them. You can say something makes sense because you want to believe the cards are telling the truth. But there's no getting around this. My recent past = anxiety. That's dead-on.

Well, that's good, I tell myself. *Because then if the reading turns out well, you'll know you have nothing to worry about.*

But if the reading turns out badly . . .

"What's the next card?" I ask. I see it's upside down.

Eve takes the book from Anna. "This is one of your three future cards. It represents the best or worst that can happen."

"Okay."

"Nine of Wands, upside down. Uh . . ."

Hastily, Eve hands the book back to Anna, who reads, "'Adversity, disaster. Ill health.'" She puts the book down. "And before you freak out, that's what *can* happen, Syd, not what is absolutely going to happen."

"And remember," says Eve, "my reading was doom and misery all the way through, but it turned out all right in the end."

I look at each of them, trying to guess how much of this is Make Syd Feel Better and how much is true.

"Next card," says Anna, obviously wanting to move on. "Future influence, something or someone who will be important to you. Knight of Wands. Huh." She peers at the book. "'Journey, advance into the unknown. Absence.'"

Absence. Sounds like loss to me. I remember "ill health." Is my dad going to have to go somewhere? Is he going to leave us?

"It's not necessarily bad," says Eve slowly. "A journey into the unknown can be a good thing."

"Yeah, but absence?"

Eve thinks. "Maybe because you're going into the unknown, you'll be absent from people you normally hang with."

"Not us, please," says Anna.

"No way," I say, even as my mom's words—*People change, new things come along. What will you do when that happens?*—echo in my head.

"What's the next card?" I ask. It's a woman, also upside down.

"This is how you see yourself. The Queen of Pentacles. Oh, Syd . . ."

"What?"

"Well, I hope this isn't how you see yourself. 'Suspicion, distrustful person, fear. Responsibilities neglected.'"

Eve throws a pillow at me. "Please tell me that's wrong."

I squirm. I don't like that description any more than Eve and Anna do. But I can't say it's false.

I explain, "That is how I feel in this situation. I don't know who to trust. I feel like I'm not doing enough, but I'm also scared that I'll screw things up by overreacting."

"That's insane," says Eve, taking the book back from Anna. "And I'll prove it. Next card, which is how people see you. Sweet, amazing, brilliant . . ."

I laugh. "Is that really what it says?"

Eve turns the page. "Uh, no." She claps the book closed. "Okay, this reading is ridiculous. I say we have a do over."

"What does it say?" I ask.

"No, we need to start again." She waves the book in the air. "Because I know for a fact this is not true. Nobody could see you like this, Syd."

My stomach clenches. "Just tell me what it says."
Sad, alone, fearful of reality . . .

"Ten of Wands." Eve reads, "'Intrigue. Deceiver. A traitor.' See? Ridiculous."

Curious, I ask, "Who sees me like that? Does it say?"

"No one, it's dumb," says Eve. "This reading is crocked."

"Let's just finish it," says Anna quietly, taking the

book back. "Next card. Hopes and fears. Two of Cups upside down . . ."

"They're all upside down," complains Eve. "I really think we did this wrong."

"Maybe," says Anna. "But let's finish it anyway." Tossing her hair back, she says, "According to this, you're afraid of false friendship, separation, divorce, crossed desires . . ."

I nod. "I am, a little."

"But false friendship? You're not afraid of losing *us*?"

Um, yes. You guys have so much good going on, all I have is family drama. But Anna's so outraged, I say, "No, not really."

"Okay, then. Because that's . . . nuts." Satisfied, Anna turns the pages. "Final card."

And for the first time, I look at the final card, my ultimate destiny. The last word on whether or not my dad will be okay.

It's Death.

I once said that the cards punish you for messing with stuff that's none of your business—and I was right. The proof is this skeleton grinning at me like, *You just had to know the future. Well, here's your worst nightmare staring you in the face.*

Instinctively, I inch away from the cards. I want to

wipe them away, pretend I never saw them. But you can't. Once you open that stupid box, you're trapped. You have the knowledge.

Her voice shaky, Anna reads, "'Loss—'"

"Stop," I tell her, "I don't want to hear it."

"But you have to know what it means."

"I know what it means," I tell her, my voice rising. "I get it. Just . . . don't . . . I don't want to hear."

"But it's not all bad," says Anna.

"Yeah, right." I stand up. "Yeah, Death is just fine. No problem. Except, oh, oops, it means someone's going to die."

I feel two seconds away from tears. But if I cry, that will make it real, so I can't cry. *They're just cards,* I tell myself fiercely, *stupid, meaningless cards. You're getting all upset over nothing.*

Eve yanks me back down, says, "This isn't necessarily what's going to happen. Things could change."

"Your reading didn't change. And, Anna? Your reading came true."

"But we wanted ours to come true," says Anna. "You don't, and you can still change the outcome."

"How?"

"Well, let's look at what leads up to . . ."—Anna doesn't want to say "death," so she substitutes—"the end result. Maybe there's something there you can change."

Change my dad, I think. *Or my mom. Yeah, that's going to work.*

Eve examines the reading. "It talks a lot about day-dreams. Like refusal to face reality."

I think of how stupid I was. *Oh, my dad's fine.* "That makes sense."

"And deception," says Anna, pointing to one of the cards.

"So maybe that's what has to change," says Eve. "People need to start dealing with reality."

I nod. "Only, I'm not sure what reality is."

Anna hesitates. "I think the reading definitely says your dad is in some kind of danger. But nobody's dealing with it, which leaves him in more danger. So maybe the first thing to do is to find out what's really going on."

I look at the last card. Anna got the Lovers, Eve got the World. I got . . . I can't even say it. I wonder if the cards can sense when you don't trust them, if they scare you to make a point. *Go ahead, say we're just cards. Boy, will you be sorry when your dad has a heart attack or a car accident.*

Eve says, "I still think we should do another reading. Too much was weird with this one."

I shake my head. As much as I'd like to agree with Eve, I asked for the truth and I got it. Once you know the truth, you have to deal with it. You have to do something. Only . . . what?

Unthinking, I reach for the Ace of Swords, love versus destruction. But Anna stops my hand and says, "Time for a sugar fix. I'm starved."

Which is just an excuse to get me away from the cards, but I troop along to the kitchen, where Anna sets out three cartons of ice cream. Plain vanilla, Cherry Garcia, and rainbow sherbet. "My family can't agree on ice-cream flavors," she explains, putting bowls on the table. "So my mom gave up and got something for everyone."

Eve inspects the sherbet. "This looks like psychedelic spew."

"That's Russell's," says Anna. "Beware boogers." Eve sets it down hastily.

For a little while everyone focuses on their ice cream. I know we're all thinking about that Death card, but no one wants to bring it up. *Death, anxiety, aloneness,* I think. *That's my future.*

Then Eve slams her spoon down on the table. "Oh. My. God. You will not believe what my moronic parents said to me last night."

"What?" says Anna.

"They said if this semester's grades aren't way

better than last semester's, they won't let me go to the audition in Philadelphia. Do you believe that?"

I do believe it—even though I know Eve's making a drama of it partly to distract me. Fine, I'll pretend to be distracted. "What are you going to do?"

"Nothing." Eve blows a raspberry. "Let my parents learn: I don't respond well to threats."

Anna says, "What about the audition?"

"They can't stop me from going."

"Um, they could not drive you," says Anna. "They could not pay for the hotel."

Eve shrugs. "I'll get McElroy to pay for it. Guys, you're forgetting the cards. According to them, my future is set. The cards cannot be wrong."

Anna shoots Eve a vicious look, hisses, "Of course they can."

Puzzled, Eve frowns. Then she realizes I need the cards to be wrong and says lamely, "Well, they're never wrong, except when . . . they . . . are."

Then she concentrates on scraping the last of the Cherry Garcia from her bowl.

That night I unleash my latest "What ifs." I force myself to think of everything that could go wrong, then try to match each disaster with something

I could do to prevent it. Like, *Disaster: Dad has car accident*—because I know you're not supposed to drink and drive. *Prevention: Don't let Dad drive.*

Disaster: Dad freaks out again and loses job. Prevention: . . .

I have no idea. Basically, my reading says I am living in a fantasy world, suspicious and mistrustful of everything, and because of this, I will end up separated and alone. . . .

And someone will die.

Beesley is curled up next to me. I pet him, feeling the bones of his spine under the skin. He needs to put on a little weight; I'll ask Liz if there's something else I can feed him.

There's a little knock on the door. At first I can't tell, Mom or Dad? Doesn't sound like either. I call, "Come in."

The door opens. Both my parents look in. My stomach lurches. This is it. The announcement. The cards even predicted it: separation, divorce.

They hesitate by the door. I say, "What?"

My mom steps aside so my dad can come in. "Your dad has something he wants to tell you."

My dad comes over and sits on the bed. My mom watches from the opposite side of the room with her arms folded. Beese senses my dad and nudges his hand with his head. My dad is one of the few other people he feels safe with.

My dad says, "Syd, I owe you an apology for what happened at the restaurant."

"Dad . . ." My mom told him to do this, I know it. I don't want to be used as her punishment.

"Hold on." My dad captures my hands in his. "I frightened you and I embarrassed you, and that's unforgivable. You have no idea how angry I am at myself."

"Don't be," I say. For some reason, I feel like my dad's always angry with himself.

"Anyone else who did that to you, I'd have serious issues with." He smiles. "So I have serious issues with myself. I apologize. It won't happen again."

There's a pause. My mom says, "Ted."

Staring at our hands, my dad says, "And . . . I'm not going to be drinking anymore. It doesn't do good things for me. Or good things to the people I love. So . . . that's something else that won't be happening again."

It's weird how you can smile and cry at the same time. How your face feels like it's cracking apart from happiness, but it must look like you're miserable because all these tears are running down your cheeks and you can't talk. But, really, it's that you're so grateful and you can't believe how lucky you are. Five minutes ago I knew my dad was going to die. Five minutes ago I knew he would be drunk and have an accident or explode from rage, and there was nothing I could do to stop it. Because the cards told me so, and the cards are never wrong, supposedly.

But Eve was right. The reading was all screwed up. The cards didn't know the most important thing.

They didn't know my dad.

FOUR

SEVEN OF CUPS
Fantasy, daydreams, wishful thinking

"Where is she?"

This is the third time Eve has asked me that question. The first two times, I said, "I don't know." Now I'm bored by that answer, so I try, "Maybe she's still finishing her test."

We're sitting in Fluff's Doughnut Shop. It's our finals ritual. The day all three of us have finished our exams and handed in our papers, we meet at Fluff's and zone out on sugar.

Only, Anna is half an hour late. I'm still working on my vanilla frosted, but Eve's on her second chocolate cruller.

"Yeah, right," says Eve scornfully. "She mumbled

something about wanting to know how Nelson's algebra test went. I bet you that's why she's late. They're making out in the park. 'Oh, darling, our finals are over! Now we can be together all summer!'" She gags.

I don't want to get into an Anna-bashing session, so I ask, "How'd *your* tests go?"

"Eh." Eve shrugs. "They went, you know? What is Shakespeare trying to say about love here? Like, I don't know. If you have to ask me, that means it isn't clear, so how great a writer can he be if no one knows what he's saying?"

Remembering Eve's parents' threat, I say, "You didn't write that, right?"

"Maybe." Eve smirks. "Nah. I gave them all the sun and moon and flowers blah-blah. Science was like, forget it. 'Define photosynthesis.' Yeah, uh, that's when a plant does something . . . kind of green. With sunlight. Again—who friggin' cares?"

Oh, boy. "But you think you did okay."

"Yeah, yeah." Eve takes another bite of cruller. "See, the way I figure, the finals are a test." Puzzled, I nod. "Not a school thing—the cards. The cards are testing me, to see how much I believe in them. And if I take my finals too seriously, it's like I don't trust the cards to deliver on their promise."

I have to hand it to Eve, that is definitely one of the most creative excuses not to study I've ever heard. When I don't say, *Oh, right! How obvious!* she changes the subject. "So, what's up with your dad?"

I pick the frosting off my doughnut while I think how to answer that. Eve has a way of questioning things to prove how worldly and cynical she is, and I don't want her getting snarky about my dad's promise to stop drinking. It's too important to me.

Still, I have to say something, since I stupidly spilled my guts. "He's been a lot better lately."

"Really?" Eve raises one eyebrow—a trick she's particularly proud of.

"Yeah." I try flattery. "I think you were right. My reading was off."

"Well, but didn't the cards also say people needed to deal with reality?" Eve licks the last of the sugar flakes from her fingers. Which annoys me. Like, *We're talking about my dad's life, and you're licking doughnut crumbs?*

I say, "How seriously are we going to take these cards? 'Ooh, the mystic cards, they foretell the future.'"

This time Eve raises both eyebrows. "Um, have to point out, I am auditioning for a major TV show."

"The cards didn't say anything about TV," I argue.

"They just said something good would happen. It was a fifty-fifty guess: good or bad."

"What about Anna getting the Lovers?"

"So she dated Declan for a few weeks. And now she's dating Nelson. Wow—big love."

"*She'd* say it was," Eve says sourly. "Romeo and Juliet time, puke."

"I'm just saying that sometimes I think you see what you want to see in the reading."

"Oh, and you *wanted* to see Death," says Eve.

"No." I flush. "But it's what I was scared of, so I got freaked out."

I know I've made Eve mad by questioning the power of the cards when her future's still up in the air—although she would never admit that—so I add, "All I mean is, you're going to be famous no matter what a bunch of cards say. They didn't make it happen, you did. You could do another reading tomorrow and it could say doom, failure—and so what? You'd still be destined to be famous, because you're really talented."

Eve frowns down at her empty plate. Then she says, "Well, I hope . . ."

Before she can say what she hopes, Anna appears at the table. At first I'm relieved, because Eve and I are close to having a fight.

But then I see Anna's not going to be much help in the peacemaking department.

For one thing, her eyes are red. For another, her mouth is tight because she's trying not to cry.

Still, she puts on a big smile and says, "Hi! How's it going?"

Then she bursts into tears.

"Okay, *what* did he say again?"

Eve is pushing a jelly doughnut at Anna. I am offering her a glass of water. Anna is crying and choking as she tries to tell us what happened with Nelson.

"He said . . ." She takes a deep breath. "He said . . ."

But she dries up. I force the water on her. "Drink this, then speak."

Anna sniffs, takes the glass. After a gulp she says, "He has to go see his grandparents . . ."

Eve rolls her eyes. "Well, that's not—"

"For the whole summer."

"But you can—"

"In Toronto."

Eve pauses. "That's, like, in another country, right?"

"Canada," I tell her. "Okay, that sucks."

Anna nods. "And he just tells me like it's no big deal. 'Oh, by the way, next week I'm leaving the country.'"

"Maybe he has to," says Eve. "Maybe the grandparent thing is a lie. He's committed some crime and—"

Stopping Eve mid-delusion, I say, "And maybe he just didn't want to hurt you, so he left it till the last minute and tried to play it like it's no big deal."

"Uh-huh," says Anna skeptically. "Well, it became a big deal, believe me."

"Why?"

"'Cause I dumped him."

There is dead silence. Until Eve says, "Way to go!" and lifts her hand for a high five. I give her a look, and she says, "Come on—guy picks Canada over you? Dump city."

Sometimes Eve's need for drama wrecks any sense of reality. I say to Anna, "You don't want to dump Nelson."

"No," she says mournfully. "Unless he's dumping me, in which case, yes."

"Anna . . ."

Sitting up straight, she says, "No, look, it's too convenient. Here we are, just a month into getting . . ." —Anna hesitates—". . . together, and all of a sudden, he's leaving? You know what I think? He couldn't handle having a girlfriend, and he decided this was the best way to get out of it."

"Makes sense," agrees Eve.

"So I made it easy for him and said fine, we're over."

There's a certain amount of sense in what Anna's saying. On the other hand, I'm pretty sure Nelson didn't mean to break up with Anna, in which case, she shouldn't be dumping him. "What about your reading? It ended with the Lovers."

"I don't know," says Anna impatiently. "Maybe the cards don't know that I'm a total dud in the romance department. Or maybe my reading ended in the Lovers but Nelson's reading would have ended in a big fat Who Cares?"

Or, I think, *maybe you dumped Nelson because Declan messed with your head and you don't want to get hurt again.*

Then I hear Anna say, "You know, maybe you *don't* get what you want in life. You have all these ideas of how everything's supposed to be, but that's just your fantasy. Like, better I learn to live with reality, right?"

There's that word again, "reality." Something about this bugs me, so I shake it off, ask, "Do you at least have his address in Toronto? Can you write to him?"

"Why should she write to him?" says Eve indignantly.

"In case things seem different tomorrow," I say through gritted teeth.

"They won't," Anna says, taking a large gulp of water.

"Look at it this way," says Eve, biting into Anna's jelly doughnut. "Now you're a free woman all summer—how fabulous is that? I bet we meet lots of great guys when we go to Philly for the audition. We have to start planning, by the way."

"I have to ask my parents, but I'm sure they'll say yes," Anna says. Then, catching sight of her red eyes and crazy hair in the wall mirror, she says, "Uck, excuse me," and heads for the bathroom.

With Anna gone, I ask Eve, "So, what do you think?"

"About the big breakup?" I nod. "Who knows? Nelson's a weird guy. Way better than Declan, but still. Maybe Anna got too intense for him, maybe he did want out. Or . . . or maybe *she* wanted out."

"Why would she want that?"

"Well, first she was with Declan, Most Wanted Boy Toy. Then she's with Superfreak? How do you think that's going down? Maybe she looked at the social humiliation angle and figured, 'End it now.' You know, who wants people going, 'Oh, my God, she's dating that loser?' Which they are, by the way. And it's only going to get worse in high school—our school is full of catty gossips."

I don't think that's how Anna thinks. If she really liked Nelson—and was sure he liked her back—no way could a pack of gossips make her break up with him. She might get too wrapped up in relationships, but she is totally and utterly loyal.

I eat the last bite of doughnut and decide not to ask Eve the other question that's on my mind: Doesn't Anna breaking up with Nelson mean her reading didn't come true after all?

So if Anna's reading didn't come true—and my reading's not coming true—will Eve's?

Coming back with her hair combed and her face washed, Anna asks Eve, "How'd your tests go?"

"Boring, boring, boring," says Eve. Slapping her hands on the table, she says, "Forget school! Starting next week, we're on vacation, baby. I hereby predict an excellent summer for all three of us."

"No more predictions," I groan.

Walking home, I try to get my head around what Anna's done. Not a single thing she said makes me think Nelson wanted to dump her—so why is she so sure he did? It's like she wants to believe it.

The human mind is such a weird thing. For instance, the way Eve believes so totally that she'll get on *Making It!* that she's not worried if she flunks her finals. I don't get how people can just decide something is true, even when there's a ton of evidence that says different.

A voice in my head grumbles, *You believe your dad, though, don't you?*

Um, yes, because he promised he wouldn't drink anymore.

Is a promise a fact?

When my dad makes it, yes.

Which feels good and strong. Like, *Ha, I believe my dad! Take that, fate!*

And somehow also feels . . . dumb.

Ugh, I wish I'd never done that dopey reading. No matter how much you tell yourself the cards are bogus, a little part of you keeps whispering, *No, they're no-ot.*

It's very simple, I tell myself. Eve and Anna believed in the cards because they told them what they wanted to hear. I don't believe in the cards because they told me what I didn't want to hear.

No, that's wrong. I don't believe in the cards because they're silly. There's no way you can prove that they foretell the future. In fact, you can prove just the opposite. Every day that my dad is okay, it shows the cards are just pieces of paper that couldn't even predict what I'll eat for breakfast tomorrow.

And how will you prove *that your dad's okay?*

In my head this voice belongs to the grinning skeleton, the nasty Death card at the end of my reading.

But my reading was wrong. The cards are silly. Ergo, I don't have to listen to them.

When I get home, I go to the kitchen and put down some food for Beesley. As he picks his way through the chow, I realize I've never left him before. Who will take care of him when I'm in Philadelphia? Because of his meds, you can't just hand him over to anyone. And my mom has made it oh so clear that she wants nothing to do with him.

There's my dad. Beese loves him. And he's seen me give Beese his meds a hundred times.

Only . . . my dad's going to start the gifted program next week. When he starts a job or a new piece, everything else disappears from his brain. That's how it is with creative people. Nothing's as real to them as their art.

The voice again: *You don't trust him. You know he's not okay.*

Which is so not true. He is okay. I'll ask him tonight.

Then, for some reason, I go to the liquor cabinet. Opening the door, I see that same bottle my dad was drinking the night he told me to go away. It was half empty then.

It's still half empty. My dad hasn't touched it. *There you go,* I think. *Proof.*

On Sunday night my dad cooks. He makes pasta primavera, which is one of my all-time favorites. My mom always makes a big thing out of the fact that I don't eat meat and that she doesn't know how to cook without it. But Dad praises each vegetable like it's a rare find he's privileged to cook with. "Look at that tomato—is that something? How fresh is this zucchini? *Bellissima.*"

Dumping a ton of grated cheese on top of her food, my mom asks, "So, how's the gifted program looking? How many kids have signed up?"

My dad shrugs. "Five, I think."

"That's not a lot," says my mom.

"How many musically gifted kids do you think there are?" my dad says with an edge in his voice. "Frankly, even the ones who have signed up are perfectly nice kids, but they're never going to play in Carnegie Hall."

"I'm sure they'll be happy to hear that," says my mom.

"I'm not going to pretend, Miranda. . . ."

That's one of Dad's sayings that gets my mom angry, so I interrupt. "Hey, speaking of art, remember how I told you Eve got picked to audition for Peter McElroy's show?"

My mom exclaims, "Not *You Suck!*" just as my dad says, "Peter who?"

I explain to my dad, "Peter McElroy hosts this talent show on TV." Then to my mom, "Not *You Suck!*, a new show. Something for musically talented kids."

The second the words are out of my mouth, I know I screwed up. Right away my mom says, "Why don't you audition?"

I improvise. "It's just for people who sing."

"You said musically talented."

"Yeah, but I meant singing." Quickly, I move on to my question. "The auditions are in Philadelphia next month, and Eve wants me and Anna to go with her for support." Anticipating the next question, I add, "Her mom will come with us, obviously. But we'd have to stay in a hotel for a few nights."

My parents glance at each other. Then my mom says, "Well, as long as it's not the Ritz. Have Eve's mom call me, okay?"

"Definitely," I say, relieved. "The thing is, someone needs to take care of Beesley. Give him his meds."

At this, my mom raises her hands like, *Don't look at me.* "Couldn't Liz board him at the clinic?"

"I don't want him in a cage alone overnight."

"Well, maybe you could ask her to take him home. Or I'll ask."

"She has two dogs, Ma. They'd freak Beesley out."

"Forget Liz," says my dad. "I can do it."

I hesitate. "I wasn't sure, since you're working this summer . . ."

"It takes time, Ted," says my mom. "And you can't miss a day, right, Syd?"

"I can handle a few days," my dad insists.

I should be saying yes right away. I hesitate, wanting to make sure my dad knows what he's getting into. Beese's meds are complicated. "It's twice a day. I don't want to screw you up."

My dad stares at me. "I'm not going to screw up." He glances from me to my mom, then back to me. "Why are the two of you acting like this?"

Something in his voice takes me back to Chez Wong. I say quickly, "If you have time, that's great. Thanks so much, Dad."

My dad gives me a long look, like he's trying to figure out if I really mean it. Then he nods. "Okay."

After dinner my mom disappears to watch *Desperate Housewives*, which is her favorite show. Why, I don't know, since we don't live in the suburbs and she's certainly not a housewife. My dad and I do the dishes.

Handing me a dish, he says, "So. This big audition of Eve's. It's for a TV show?" My dad makes a face like the word "TV" tastes bad.

"Yeah—*Making It!* Peter McElroy runs a record company, and if you win, you get a contract."

My dad nods sharply. "And he thinks thirteen-year-olds are ready for this kind of pressure."

I have no idea what Peter McElroy thinks, but I say, "Well, lots of people start young. Christina Aguilera . . ."

"I don't know who that is."

"She's, um . . ." There's nothing I can say about Christina Aguilera that will mean anything to my dad. "Anyway, you started young, didn't you?"

"Not on TV. Not for people who weren't qualified to judge whether I was any good or not. And not pop garbage where they digitally alter your voice so it doesn't matter if you have talent or not."

I hate when my dad gets like this, insisting that anyone who sings stuff you hear now can't be any good. "Eve is talented."

"Then she should stay away from people like Peter McElroy." He throws a spoon in the drying rack. It misses and clatters into the sink. "God—why do we push these kids? Compete, compete, compete. Be good, be better, be best. Best according to whom? You go crazy trying to make people like you, do what they want. It's all so phony."

Somehow we're not talking about Eve anymore. In fact, *we're* not talking at all. It's like my dad's forgotten I'm here. My stomach twists up. Taking the spoon out of the sink, I run it under water, concentrating on getting it clean, until I hear, "All I'm saying is, I hope Eve doesn't get hurt."

I can tell from his voice, my dad is back. Smiling, I say, "I know. I'll try to keep her somewhat sane."

My dad picks up a pot, starts scrubbing it. "That's why I never wanted that for you. Music camp, competitions, all that stuff your mom pushes. Julliard, for God's sake. I don't want you exposed to all that criticism and judgment."

"I know, Daddy." I almost never call my dad "Daddy" anymore. But every once in a while, when I want to show I really love him, I do.

Later I go to take out the garbage. But my dad says, "That's okay, sweetie, I got it."

That night I flip through my dad's scrapbook. In one picture my dad's a teenager, sitting at the piano with Leonard Bernstein behind him. Leonard Bernstein was the greatest conductor in the world at the time. For him to notice my dad was a big deal. My dad looks so young, his hair short and slicked over to the side, big smile, dark eyes bright and happy.

All that criticism and judgment.

I would never tell Eve this, but my dad knows what he's talking about with the music world. I'm glad he fights my mom about music camp and competition, because otherwise, I'd be going to all of them and having twelve nervous breakdowns a day. He knows how harsh people can be or how disappointing it is when everyone says how great you are, but it doesn't work out. That's why he flipped out when Mr. Courtney wanted me to try for Julliard. He wasn't too crazy about me playing piano for Eve's musical in the first place.

But that worked out okay, actually. Based on what Eve and Anna say about their school, I was worried people would be nasty, but everyone was so nice. Especially Mr. Courtney. Still, I think my dad's right. Julliard's not for me.

I hear a door open—the one to my parents' bedroom. Someone coming down the hall.

It's my dad. The floorboards always creak when it's him. My mom's rat-a-tat-tat doesn't give the floor a chance.

I listen. He's going to the kitchen.

In my mind I see that grinning skeleton from the Death card. He turns to face me, hisses, *Don't worry,*

Syd. Your dad's not drinking. He's just wandering around the house in the middle of the night.

Struggling, I try to focus on the facts. Fact: There is still half a bottle of scotch left. If my dad were drinking, it'd be gone.

I hear thuds in the kitchen, cabinet doors opening and closing.

Get up, Syd. You're so sure? Just get out of bed, go to the kitchen. Go on and see for yourself. You want facts? They're right down the hall.

My dad's coming back. The door to his bedroom creaks open, closes.

The next morning I go to the kitchen and check that the bottle is still there, still half empty.

Just to make sure.

FIVE

NINE OF SWORDS

Concern, anxiety over a loved one

And it's still there the next day. And the next day and the day after that. After a while I don't know why I check the cabinet anymore. It's become some kind of weird ritual. As long as that bottle is there, the cards are wrong and my dad is all right.

On the morning he starts the gifted program, I make sure I'm up early. Always, on the first day of work, I wish my dad luck. It started the first time he lost his job and had to start at a new school. I was, like, eight, and I ran up to him at the door and yelled, "Good luck, Daddy!" or something stupid. But I guess he liked it, because ever since, on the first day of school, he says, "Need that good luck."

So when my dad comes down the hall dressed in what he calls his "teacher suit," I call out, "Good luck!"

My dad stops, gives me this funny little salute. "Think I can handle it?"

Without thinking, I say, "Of course." Then, "Are you worried?"

My dad shrugs a little. "Eh, you know. Kids like to test, show you they know more than you—especially the 'gifted' ones." Then he points to me. "Don't forget, we have a lesson this afternoon."

Which is a joke, because I have never once missed a lesson. "I won't forget," I say solemnly.

That afternoon I go sit in the living room to wait for my dad to come home. The sheet music is already set up on the piano. I have this superstition that I can't open the book until my dad is here. But I can't help splitting the pages with my thumb and taking a peek. A swirl of black and white, music waiting to happen, like spirits floating in the air. My hands feel ready; I want to hear the music, even if I make mistakes.

When I hear the key turn in the lock, I half get up from the bench, then sit back down. I don't want to run to my dad going, *How was it?* That's what my mom would do.

But when he comes into the living room, his suit jacket still on, I can tell it didn't go great. If it went great, my dad would come busting into the room, clap his hands, and say, *Okay, who's ready for Schumann?* Instead, he sits down, leans his head back, and shuts his eyes. He must have seen me when he came in, but I'm not certain he knows I'm here.

For a moment I feel forgotten. Then I tell myself not to be so selfish. I ask, "Would you like a cup of tea, Dad?"

He says in a thin, tired voice, "That'd be nice, sweetie. Thank you."

As I make the tea, Beesley creeps around my legs. I tell him we have to understand if Dad's tired. Teaching is one of the hardest jobs in the world—especially when you care, maybe even too much, the way Dad does. Carrying the tea in one hand, I scoop Beesley up with the other, go back to the living room.

I set the tea down on the table next to my dad's chair. "Are they testing?"

My dad sighs. "Oh, yeah."

I imagine these kids, laughing, making dumb jokes, pretending to listen. I don't know why some kids have to fight the teacher. I hate it when Eve makes fun of teachers. I want to say, *You think it's easy? You try it. You get to make fun of them, laugh at them. You think they don't know you do that? You think they don't go home feeling lousy? Well, guess what, they do.*

I say, "It'll get better, Daddy."

He opens his eyes, smiles a little. "I know. First day's always tough."

Then he takes my hand. "Hey, can we maybe start the lessons tomorrow? Old man's a little ragged."

I feel a thud of disappointment, a sneaky, ugly feeling that if I had any real talent, my dad wouldn't put me off like this.

The Death card whispers: *It won't be tomorrow. It won't be the next day, either. Because it's not going to get better, Sydney. No matter what you believe . . .*

Shutting that voice off, I say, "Sure, Daddy, I understand."

That night I'm half asleep when I hear the creak of my parents' door opening. I wait for the click of the bathroom light, the sound of the toilet, but they don't come.

Instead, footsteps. Down the hall.

I should get up. Get up and tell my dad not to do this. That bottle won't make his students easier or my mom more understanding or . . . that something he wants but can't quite have.

Then I tell myself, *He's not having a drink. He's just walking around because he can't sleep. He promised.*

Still, the next day I check the cabinet. The bottle's the same. I feel hugely relieved.

That afternoon I get my report card. I set it on the piano, because my dad always likes to see it. (He often makes fun of the comments, particularly the ones that say, *Sydney must speak up more.* "Right," he says, "because it means I, the teacher, have to speak less and can read the newspaper.")

As I wait for my dad to arrive, I tell myself I can't be disappointed if he comes home and says, *Ugh, sorry, can't today.* Really, we were silly to start this summer's lessons at the same time he started his new teaching assignment. But that's my dad—he always wants to do everything, even when he can't.

At 3:15 I tell myself he's probably talking to one of his students.

At 3:45 I tell myself he's on his way home.

At 4:00 I get up from the piano, because if I'm still sitting there when my dad walks in, it'll feel like a criticism.

At 4:15 I wonder what'll happen if he doesn't come home. Then I wonder what'll happen if he doesn't come home while I'm in Philadelphia.

At 4:25 I tell myself to quit thinking that.

At 4:30 he walks through the door. "I'm sorry, honey."

"That's okay, Dad."

The next day I don't wait at the piano.

That night at dinner my mom asks how the program is going. My dad shrugs, says, "It's going."

My mom asks, "What are the students like?"

My dad's mouth tightens. I say, "You said they were great, right, Dad? Really promising."

My dad nods over his plate. "Some of them."

My mom gives me a long look like she knows something is up. I feel guilty about lying to her, but she doesn't need to know; she'd only overreact and make things worse. To her, if things are difficult, it's because you're making them difficult. She either doesn't get that there are selfish, rude people in the world or she doesn't care. And frankly, sometimes I think that's because she can be a selfish, rude person herself.

When my mom's not looking, my dad smiles at me in gratitude. I smile back.

As we're clearing the dishes, the phone rings. Putting a hand to his forehead like a fortune-teller, my dad says, "I see a girl on the phone, a dark girl with spiky hair. Or wait—maybe brown hair. There's trouble, she needs help. Only Sydney can help her."

"Dad . . ." Grinning, I go to pick up the phone. I barely have time to say "Hello?" when Eve shrieks over the line, "I hate them! I'll hurt them! I can't believe they're doing this to me!"

I say, "Whoa, wait, what's happened?"

"My stinky . . . rotten . . . heinous . . . *evil* parents . . ."

"What'd they do?"

"I got my report card, right?" Oh, no. "And now they say I can't audition for the show! Can you believe that? I get one stupid D, and the fact that I did better in every other subject doesn't matter. I *hate* them!"

Oh, God. I was so afraid this would happen. And yet, why do I also feel strangely thrilled?

Trying to focus on Eve, I say, "You did better in everything else?"

"Yes! Like Bs. Maybe a C. Like . . . two."

"What does the school say?"

"Even the school is being cooler than they are, okay? They say as long as I get a tutor and study over the summer, it's fine. But my parents are all like, 'You're going into ninth grade next year, your grades really count, college, blah-blah-blah, you don't have your priorities straight.' And I'm like, 'Yes, I do! Only they're not *your* priorities!' College? Hello—I'm thirteen!"

I try to think. How can we get Eve's parents to back down? If Eberly is willing to take her back, I bet part of the reason her parents are being so hard on her is they know she didn't take their threat seriously. So, what can Eve do to make them think she does take it seriously?

"I'm running away," she announces. "If they don't let me go, I'll get there myself, I don't care. Can I borrow five hundred bucks?"

This was not what I had in mind.

"Wait," I tell her. "We can figure this out. Have you told Anna?"

"Not yet."

"Call Anna." Anna is the absolute queen of dealing with grown-ups. She always knows what they want to hear. If anyone can figure out the right strategy for Eve, it's Anna.

The next day we're sitting in Fluff's, and Anna is thinking hard. Eve and I are watching her think. Finally, Eve bangs a spoon on the table, says, "So?"

Anna sighs. "Okay, was it both your parents or just your dad who said you couldn't go?"

"My mom's such a wuss, she says anything my dad does."

"But do you think she actually agreed with him? Or was it just a united front thing?" Anna explains. "Like—if you went to her separately and said, 'Mom, this is *so* important to me, I will do *anything* you say if you let me go . . .'"

94

"Whoa," says Eve, "anything?"

"You're desperate," says Anna. "You have to say 'anything.'" She looks to me for support, and I nod. "If you did that, do you think she might talk your dad into it?"

"Hmm—maybe. I don't know, though. He's a crazy person."

"What if," I suggest, "you make a promise? Something she can say to your dad, something new."

"I promised to buy him a new house when I got famous. What more does he want?"

"More than a D in math," says Anna reasonably. "You have to consider how he sees this. He wants to hear that you're just as upset about your grades as he is." Eve snorts. "Well, fake it," Anna continues. "Pretend you've really thought about it and you want to do better. Then tell him what you're going to do to try."

Eve thinks. "Run Ms. Frobisher over with a bus and get a new teacher who doesn't make me want to throw up?"

Anna and I look at each other, take deep breaths. Anna says, "It doesn't matter what you offer to do, just act like school is really important to you. Say 'I'm sorry' a million times."

"Not a million," I put in. "That won't sound

genuine. Just once or twice, sounding really sincere." Anna nods in agreement.

"But it's not important to me," Eve protests. "I couldn't care less."

Frustrated, I say, "You're an actress, right?" Eve nods. "So act."

"Say you want to stay at Eberly with me," says Anna. "So they think it's a friend thing."

Eve nods. "I can pull that off."

"And don't be angry when you talk to your mom. Get her on your side."

"Be really sad," I urge. "'I'm sorry, I'm so sorry, I feel terrible . . .'"

Eve groans. "Can't I just run away?"

"No," says Anna firmly. "Do it tonight and call us afterward."

"Okay," Eve huffs. Kicking the table, she says, "The cards better not let me down."

And that's when I realize why I've had this odd sense of hope ever since Eve told me her parents might not let her go to the audition. Because it's not enough for me that Anna's reading didn't come true. I don't want Eve's to come true either. That way, I'll know my dad is safe.

What kind of awful person am I? Being a successful singer is the most important thing in the world to

Eve, and this audition gives her a real shot. I would wish for her not to get it, just so I can be sure my reading won't come true?

Don't I have enough proof? That bottle sitting in the cabinet, untouched all this time?

The Death card appears in my head, sneers, *And your dad promised . . .*

The cards warned me about not dealing with reality. But I am dealing with reality. Every day I check the cabinet. But maybe checking the cabinet isn't enough?

I need something else that's real. Something rational and scientific. Not some magical cards that supposedly tell the future. I need facts. So on the way home from Fluff's, I stop at the library. When I was little, my dad brought me here all the time. He was the only dad there, most of the time. Everyone else had moms or nannies. He used to sit on the floor of the children's room, alongside all the kids and stuffed animals, and we'd read *Mrs. Piggle-Wiggle.* I loved *Mrs. Piggle-Wiggle,* all those crazy candies and syrups she had to cure obnoxious kids—although my dad said it was complete fantasy.

I go the computer section, but every computer is occupied. The guy at the help desk says it'll be an hour's wait. I take a number, then go to the teen section and look for books on . . .

I'm not even sure. Crazy parents? Angry dads?

He had too much.

No more drinking, I swear.

I search the teen section for books on what to do when one of your parents may be an alcoholic. But every book I look at—every single one—tells me what to do about *my* alcoholism. Only one book is about parents who are drug addicts. Maybe nobody does books anymore about people who are only a little screwed up. Maybe there aren't enough of us anymore—you're either normal or majorly crazy.

Still, because I've got forty-five minutes before my computer time, I go to the adult part of the library and scan the health section. This is better. Nothing on parents who are alcoholics, but tons of books on drinking and what to do if your spouse is an alcoholic. Looking around, I take one of those down and open it. At the very beginning I find what I've been looking for: a checklist of symptoms.

Do you lose time from work due to drinking?

That's a no. Only . . . sometimes my dad gets sick and stays home from work. But everybody does, don't they? Although, he never really seems to have a cough or anything like that. Could it be from drinking? In my head I answer, *Maybe.*

Do you drink every day?

Several weeks ago that would have gotten an immediate yes. Now it gets . . . an *I don't know*.

No, it gets a no. A definite no.

Do you have trouble stopping drinking, even though you've tried?

I slam the book shut. Why isn't there anything that'll just say, *Yeah, your dad's a drunk* or *Quit worrying already!*

Then I hear, "Hey."

Immediately, I wrap my arms around the book, hide the cover against my shirt. At the end of the row is Mark Baylor.

I manage a "Hey" as I wonder if there's a way I can get the book back onto the shelf without him noticing.

Then I get an idea. "I'm doing a summer project for school." I hold up the book. "Addiction. The deep and terrible secret."

Mark nods once. "Oh, yeah, I remember that project. I got sexually transmitted diseases. I mean, *I* didn't get . . ."

If anything, Mark is even cuter when he blushes. I smile. "I guess I was lucky to get addiction."

I should let him go. Right now, before I have a chance to make a fool of myself. But I can't resist saying, "I just saw Eve."

Mark makes a face. "Let me guess, she's running away from home."

"You know about the fight?"

"How could I not know? The whole building knows, probably the whole neighborhood. Believe me, when my family fights, everybody knows about it."

I have a flash of my family in the restaurant, people turning and staring. "Sounds pretty yucky."

"One word for it."

There's a pause. Frantic, I try to think of something to say, something to ask, anything to keep this conversation going. Then I hear, "Forty-three? Number forty-three?"

My number. My computer's free. Why is it always that the moment you get one thing you want, you lose something else?

"That's me," I tell Mark.

He blinks. "You're using a library computer? Don't you have one at home?"

"Yes, of course," I say defensively, not adding, *I didn't want my parents knowing what I was looking up.* "But I figured, as long as I'm here . . ."

"Number forty-three?" Louder this time.

"Their system is Stone Age," warns Mark. "You know how to use it?" I hesitate, and he says, "I'll show you."

Okay. Another truth learned. Sometimes you get exactly what you want—Mark continuing to remain in my presence—only, instead of being great, it's humiliating. I don't want to be some little girl he has to "show" how to do things. Why can't I say, *Ah, yes, the so-and-so system, I know the blah-blah program quite well.* . . .

At the station Mark steps up to the computer, clucks disapprovingly at the screen. "Yeah, see . . ." He types in some code, checks the screen, then steps back. "There, you're ready to go."

Determined to prove I know what I'm doing, I type *"alcoholism"* + *"parents"* on the keyboard. As the computer searches, I turn to Mark and say, "Thanks. I got it."

He has a peculiar look on his face. Maybe he's not used to me telling him to get lost. I feel a small surge of triumph. Awkwardly, he says, "Okay. Cool."

"Yeah," I say as casually as possible. "Thanks."

Mark starts to leave, then suddenly turns. "If you ever want any more help, figuring stuff out? Let me know."

Wow, okay. All those stupid advice columns that say *Play it cool,* maybe they know what they're talking about. I guess it makes sense. Who wants someone who grovels after them, like, *Oh, pay attention to me, please, please, just one kind little word* . . .

Resolved: Play it cool with Mark from now on.

Realization: It doesn't matter if I play it cool or not. Mark is never going to regard me as girlfriend material.

Still, it was fun to see him feel foolish for once.

The Internet is so huge, it's hard to know what to focus on first. So I just print anything that looks sort of relevant. Twenty minutes later, when the computer guy calls, "Time!" I have several articles. On the way home I stop at a Jamba Juice and sort through what I have. Terms like "incoherent," "raging," "blackout" jump out at me. Some of it sounds like my dad, but a lot of it sounds like someone who's really sick. Crazy sick. Like, there would be no question that there was something wrong with this person.

All these facts, and I feel like I'm no closer to the truth than I was before.

Sighing, I put the papers back in my bag. I can't think about this anymore. So for a little while I imagine that Mark is sitting next to me. I hand him the printouts. He reads them and says, *Don't worry about this stuff.* Then he opens the window and lets them all blow away.

As I head home, I realize that I'm late for my lesson. Or I would be, if we had ever started. But I feel rotten. If my dad's home, it'll feel like I'm telling him,

Oh, I give up, I know you're never going to come through.
Which I don't think at all.

Maybe that's why, when I open the door, something feels strange. I look for Beesley; usually, the sound of the door brings him out of hiding. But he's nowhere. Standing by the door, I call, "Hello?"

No answer. I try, "Anyone home? Beese? Dad?"

This time I hear from the kitchen, "Yeah, I'm here."

My dad's voice sounds strange. Like someone has a knife to his throat. I don't know whether to go back there or not. What if it's a burglar with a gun? *Don't be dumb,* I tell myself. If it were a burglar, my father would tell me to get out of the house. I call, "Are you okay?"

There's a long, long pause. Now I'm getting scared.

Then my dad says, "I'm just . . . I'm just here."

I go directly back to the kitchen. My dad is sitting at the table, his fists on his knees. Beese is crouched under the table, watching him with huge eyes.

I say, "What happened? What's wrong?"

For a moment he doesn't speak. He just stares down at his hands. Then he says, "I hate them."

"Who?"

He shakes his head, pounds his leg with his fist. He's shaking. My dad is shaking.

"Who, Daddy?"

He punches his leg again, and I feel like he's really going to hurt himself. Like he's going to start hitting himself and never be able to stop.

"I don't know . . ."

"What?"

"I don't know if I can do this."

"It's okay," I whisper. Meaning if he can't do this.

I say it all, so he understands. "It's okay if you can't do this."

And that's when he starts to cry.

This is what my dad looks like when he cries. The fists open up and he starts rubbing his legs over and over again with the palms of his hands. It's mostly air, gasping like he can't breathe. His mouth is open and stiff like someone rammed a bar between his teeth and it really hurts. His eyes are closed like he can't stand to see himself.

Every once in a while, he makes a sound, a real crying sound, and I don't know where it comes from, but it's awful. It makes me want to run out of the room.

Which I can't do. I just stand there and pat his arm. I'm afraid to hug him. Like, too much pressure and he'll explode.

Then I notice my dad is staring at the cabinet.

The one that has the bottle. I say, "I'll get you some water."

For a moment it seems like he didn't hear me. Then he says, "Yeah, thanks." Taking a deep breath, he says, "Oh, boy."

Handing him a glass, I say, "Feel better?"

"Yes." He sits up straighter. "Yes, I do. I guess sometimes . . ."

". . . you have to throw a chair."

He laughs. "I guess you do." He leans down to address Beesley. "Hope I didn't worry you, Beesley, my friend." Beesley creeps out, allows my dad to pick him up. I smile. He's so sweet, he always knows when someone needs him.

"We'll be okay," says my dad, stroking his ears. "Even when our girl's gone for a few days, we'll be fine, right, Beese? Hey." He looks at me. "How about I do a trial run with his meds?"

"That'd be great," I say.

"You watch now."

"I will."

And I do watch, very closely. But my dad does it perfectly. He starts by rubbing Beesley's head, cupping it in his palm and stroking his forehead with his thumb. Beese closes his eyes, a sign that he's happy and relaxed. I feel a rush of gratitude. If my dad wasn't doing this, I'd have to board Beesley, and at his age, I'm not sure he could take it.

Besides, my dad needs something to feel good about right now. My dad needs to feel like people are on his side. Otherwise, he'd be like Beesley. He'd retreat to his hiding place and wouldn't come out.

As he puts Beese's meds away, he says casually, "Do me a favor, don't tell your mother about this."

That night Eve calls. "It worked!" she says. "My parents totally caved. My dad wasn't thrilled, but Mom said three little days weren't going to make any difference as long as I studied the rest of the summer."

I'm quiet as I register the fact that Eve's reading is now back on target. And who's to say Nelson won't call Anna from Canada? Her reading isn't necessarily kaput either. Both their readings could still come true.

But mine won't, I tell myself.

SIX

QUEEN OF PENTACLES, UPSIDE DOWN
Suspicion, fear, responsibilities neglected

I don't tell my mom about what happened that afternoon. And I don't tell Anna and Eve, either. By now I know better. They'll try to make a huge deal out of it. But people get upset. It's not the end of the world.

And it's easy not to tell people things when one of them is super obsessed with her upcoming audition and the other one is super depressed about her possible ex-boyfriend. Eve wants to make sure her performance is perfect, so we've started rehearsing at my house. Which is a little tough because with the pressure of the audition, Eve has gone into Evil Eve mode and since Nelson left for Toronto, Anna's been about as cheerful as a broken umbrella.

One afternoon I'm banging out "Don't Tell Mama," which is the song from *Cabaret* that Eve will be singing, when she snaps her fingers impatiently and says, "Nah, nah, we got to do something different."

I glance at Anna to see what she thinks of this latest attack of diva-itis. But she's moodily flipping through one of my mom's decorating magazines.

I take a deep breath. "Like what?"

"I don't know," says Eve. "We've got to make it more now. Not so old-fashioned."

"It's from an old musical," says Anna. "How 'now' can it sound?"

"Well, we have to find a way," says Eve stubbornly. "I can't go in there sounding old."

"Isn't this what Peter McElroy asked you to sing?" I remind her.

"I can't rely on that," says Eve. "I need to have everything . . ."—her hands flex in the air like they're looking for the word—". . . perfect, foolproof."

"What about the cards?" says Anna, fake innocent. "I'm sure they'll make it all come out right."

Eve glares. She knows Anna's hurting, but she wants to hit back anyway.

To distract her, I say, "What if we change the tempo a little?" I play a bit of the song at a faster speed. "Does that help?"

Eve starts singing along, then says, "No, that's not it."

We play with various arrangements, but none of them satisfy. Then Eve decides she's had enough and her voice needs to rest. Flopping down on the couch, she says, "Okay, guys, help me figure out what to wear."

This is the ninety-third discussion of what Eve is going to wear. The reason it's the ninety-third discussion is that she's rejected every idea Anna and I have come up with so far. Anna sighs and picks up the magazine again.

Hastily, I say, "I still think you should go with something comfortable."

"Aka boring," says Eve. "No way. I have to stand out." She looks to Anna, awaiting input. Anna makes a big show of turning the page. I rack my brains for another suggestion but can't come up with one that hasn't already been turned down.

Anna turns another page.

Eve says, "You know, when certain people were trying to come up with a new look to win the hottie of their dreams, certain other people spent a lot of time and effort helping them."

This is a dangerous reminder of Declan—the hottie Anna was trying to win. Anna peers over the top of the magazine, says, "Maybe certain people weren't doing certain other people the big fat favor they thought they were."

"Well," Eve shoots back, "it's not certain people's fault that the hottie in question turned out to be a jerk."

I break in. "Guys, let's not—"

Anna throws the magazine on the floor. "Let's not what? Act like there's anyone in the universe except Eve? Acknowledge that maybe some of us have other things to worry about than some *stupid* audition?"

"Or some *stupid* boyfriend in Toronto?" snaps Eve.

Before things get totally crazed, I bring both hands down on the piano. A jangle of chords booms into the room. You're never supposed to do that, it's bad for the piano, but I figure, desperate times . . .

And it works. Both Eve and Anna stop, look at me. "Now," I say, "how about we get back to the music?"

I start playing. But as I do, I remember the card that predicted crossed desires and separation. Then the other that mentioned a journey, but also absence.

What if . . . we're not all still friends by the end of this trip?

Forget the reading, I think. *Just play.*

✳

The night before we leave, I'm packing in my room. It's only three days and three nights, so I don't need that much. But somehow it seems like I've put every piece of clothing I own on the bed to be packed. Not to mention my iPod, the Schumann sheet music, and my "Essential Creatures" scrapbook, which has pictures of my dad, my mom, Liz, Anna, Eve, and all my animals, from Bluey, my goldfish when I was three, to Beesley.

There's a knock at the door. I call, "Yeah?"

My mom comes in. She looks at the mess on the bed. I say, "Don't worry, I'm not taking everything."

"I'm sure you have things perfectly in hand," says my mom. She sits carefully on the edge of my squashy chair. Usually, Beese is there, but with all the packing commotion, he's by my feet, keeping an eye on me.

My mom says, "Seems like he doesn't want to let you out of his sight."

"Yeah," I admit. "He's a little nervous."

My mom rubs the worn arm of the chair. "Honey, there's still time to leave him with Liz."

I drop a pair of flip-flops in my suitcase. "Mom."

"I just think this is asking a lot of your father right now."

"He wants to do it."

"Yes, but he has other issues that need attention.

Have you thought of what will happen if he can't come directly home after school?"

Yes—but my mom doesn't need to know that. "He says he has no meetings."

"What if something comes up?"

Frustrated, I say, "It's just for three days, Mom."

"I'm thinking of you, Sydney, most of all."

"Well, don't," I snap. "Think about Dad. Think about how it would feel to him if I said, 'I don't trust you to deal with this.'"

"All right, all right." My mom puts her hands up. "I can't fight you both."

When she's gone, I throw my two least favorite shirts in the bag. I don't get my mom. How can she not see how mean she can be when she thinks she's trying to do "good"?

And the worst thing is, I was just about okay with leaving. Now I feel like a nervous wreck. Sitting on the bed with my bag half packed, I try to fight the feeling that this trip is jinxed. Something about it feels wrong, like all the signs are pointing to *Disaster! This Way!*

If I leave, something bad will happen, I know it.

Oh, yeah, like what, Sydney? Don't be such a scaredy-cat.

I look at Beese, staring anxiously up at me. If anything happened to him . . .

Then I remember my mom's words: *This is asking a*

lot of your father right now. Like he's sick or something. But he's not. He's fine. And he'd hate it if we treated him any other way.

And you know he's fine because . . . ? the hateful voice hisses.

Because I do. Because the bottle is still there. Because you're cards, not reality. Go away!

The next morning I give Beese a long cuddle. I tell him all about the trip, how I'll be thinking about him every second and that I'll be back very soon. I stroke his thin, fragile body, look into his huge, patient eyes, then set him down.

Standing at my door, my dad says gently, "Remember. Be patient. Twice a day. I haven't forgotten."

"Call me? If anything goes wrong?"

He smiles. "What if nothing goes wrong?"

Looking at his smiling face, his big, strong hands, I think, *Right, Sydney. Nothing will go wrong. Happy, normal people know this. Nightmares aren't real, your worst fears don't come true. Good things come true. Eve is going to be a big star. Anna will find a new boyfriend. And none of the things you're so scared of are going to happen.*

I give my dad the biggest hug. "Thanks again, Dad. For taking care of Beese."

"Sure thing."

"And take care of yourself."

He frowns a little at this, then says, "Go. You'll be late."

There's a massive crowd in front of Eve's building, and for a split second I think it's a TV crew, filming the beginning of her great journey. Then I realize it's just Eve, her mom, her dad, two doormen, and a ton of luggage.

And Mark. At the sight of him, I feel a lurch of hope.

Eve is yelling at her mom, "I can't put anything back! This is all absolutely, totally necessary. I won't know what to wear until I see what other kids are wearing."

"I thought this was a singing competition," says Mark, "not a fashion show."

As Mr. Baylor tries to stuff all of Eve's things into the trunk, Eve waves at the building and shouts, "Ciao, old pathetic life. Hello, fabulous new one."

Mark rolls his eyes. "At least try to stay in the realm of reality."

"This is reality," snaps Eve. "Everything up until now has been a hideous nightmare."

Mr. Baylor closes the trunk with a triumphant slam. Then he turns to Eve and says, "Now—"

But Eve cuts him off, saying, "Yeah, yeah, I'm not

going to make it, it's a total long shot, blah-blah-blah."

"Something like that." Her dad hugs her. "Be good to your mother." Mrs. Baylor, who's already in the car, lifts her eyes to heaven.

Eve bounds into the backseat. Then Anna gets in next to her. Mr. Baylor, Mark, and I are left standing on the street. Stupidly, I say to Mark, "Well, bye."

"Good luck," says Mark.

"You should say that to Eve," I tell him.

"You're dealing with Eve," he says. "You need all the luck you can get."

"I heard that!" Eve yells, hanging out the window. "Syd, come on!"

As I get in the car, Eve shouts to the doormen, "Bye, Juan. Bye, Pablo. Hey, when I'm famous, you want to be my bodyguards? I'll triple your salary!"

"Buckle up, everyone," says Mrs. Baylor.

And we're off.

As we cross the river to New Jersey, Eve explains the schedule to us. Today she has to register for the audition. Tomorrow is the audition to get into the audition. Then the next day is the real audition for Peter McElroy and the other judges.

"That's what they show on TV," she explains. "The

audition where they say either 'No thanks' or, in my case, 'See you in September!'"

"September?" The car swerves as Eve's mom glances at her.

"That's when the show starts filming."

"You didn't tell us that," says Mrs. Baylor.

"I totally did, Mom." I wonder if Mrs. Baylor knows that when Eve holds her eyes wide open like that, she's lying.

Apparently, she does, because she says, "Don't lie to me, Eve. At no point did you reveal that particular piece of information."

"Well, I'm revealing it now," Eve says blandly.

"Well," says Mrs. Baylor, "we'll cross that road when we come to it."

"What does that mean?" Eve demands.

"It means . . . we'll cross that road."

As I listen to them argue, I think how strange it would be if Eve manages to win over Peter McElroy, the other judges, even the whole world—everyone except her parents.

When we get to Philadelphia, Eve insists we go straight to the Constitution Center. No lunch, no bathroom, no nothing. At first I think, *Oh, great, more drama queen behavior.* But then I see the line of contestants waiting to register. It's endless, stretching all the way through the lobby of the building, out onto the street, down the block, and around the corner. This is possibly the most people I have ever seen in one place.

At the sight of such a mob, Mrs. Baylor goes limp. "Don't tell me we have to wait on that. Can't we tell someone you know Peter McElroy?"

"Mom," says Eve quickly, "why don't you go to the hotel? We'll call you when we're done and you can pick us up."

Mrs. Baylor looks at Eve, then back at the line. "Are you sure?"

"Totally sure."

Mrs. Baylor hesitates, then decides even Eve can't get into much trouble standing on line. Stern, she says, "If you're not done by nightfall, I'm coming to get you. Don't even think you're sleeping here, young lady."

A shadow crosses Eve's face. Clearly, that's what she was thinking. But she opens her eyes wide and says, "Coolio."

"Okay," says Mrs. Baylor. "Hot bath, here I come."

When Mrs. Baylor has left, Eve says, "I may have to kill her."

"You can't," says Anna. "She's our ride home."

I ask a sweet-faced, pudgy girl ahead of us how

long she thinks the wait will be. Leaning sideways to look up the line, she guesses, "A few hours? It's moving pretty fast."

Eve narrows her eyes. "What do you do? Sing, dance—what?"

"Singing."

The death ray intensifies. "Oh, *really*. Me too."

The girl nods. "A lot of us are singers. Also, a lot of people I talked to are singing Whitney Houston songs. Like, even the guys. But I'm doing gospel, so I figure maybe I'll stand out a little. What are you singing?"

Eve hesitates, not sure whether to share this important piece of information. Then I guess she realizes the girl can't steal her song at this point, and she says, "I'm doing a show tune."

"See, now that's smart," says the girl. "You'll be different, they'll like that. By the way, I'm Caroline."

Nothing melts Eve like praise. She lifts a hand. "Eve."

Hours of waiting on line can turn the deadliest rivals into friends. Eve and Caroline chat away about *You Suck!* contestants, what they think the show is really looking for, how it's fixed in favor of some people and against others. I turn to Anna, about to suggest we take a juice break. But she's checking her phone for messages.

Which reminds me to check my phone. No messages. For a moment I think of calling home. But we just left a few hours ago. What's my dad going to think? I don't even trust him for a few hours? I put my phone back in my bag.

After what feels like an eternity, we finally trudge inside the building. At the registration table we're given a packet of information and two pieces of paper with a number on it—1454. This is Eve's official number, the lady tells us. If we lose it, Eve doesn't exist as far as *Making It!* is concerned. Eve gives the piece of paper a kiss, leaving a lipstick imprint. "This," she says, "will be worth something one day."

As we're leaving, Caroline calls out, "Good luck!"

"Don't need it," says Eve cheerfully. "But thanks!"

Anna calls Mrs. Baylor to come pick us up. As we drive back to the hotel, Mrs. Baylor says, "Sweetie, you know this is a long shot, right?"

"Not for me, it's not."

"Just . . . I don't want you to feel you have to get in to prove anything to me and your dad."

She reaches across the front seat to touch Eve's shoulder, but Eve jerks away. "I'm not proving anything to you. I'm proving it to"—her arm sweeps through the air—"the world."

I have a sudden vision of the picture of my dad as

a baby sitting at the piano. On impulse, I tell Eve, "I think what your mom means is, we know you're amazing no matter what."

"Well, that's swell," says Eve. "But I want the whole country to know it too."

At the hotel Anna and I have one room and Eve and her mother have another. We're in our pajamas and I'm brushing my teeth when there's a knock on the door. Anna opens it, and Eve comes in with her pillow. "I'm sleeping with you guys," she says. "My mom's driving me nuts."

I spit and rinse. "How so?"

"Oh . . ." Eve flops angrily onto my bed. "'Don't be too disappointed if it doesn't work out. There's a lot of competition and you're very young.' All that garbage. I finally said, 'Why don't you admit you think I have no shot?'"

"She's just doing the mom thing," says Anna.

"Well, it's making me *insane*." Standing up on the bed, she starts jumping on it. "Insane, insane, *insane*."

Eve shouts the last "insane." Nervous that the people next door will bang on the wall, I say, "What's the first thing you'll buy when you're a big success?"

Eve's eyes glitter. She loves this game. Settling down on the bed, she says, "Okay, first thing . . . first thing . . . oh, well, my own place. Definitely. Farewell parents and Marky Mark."

Lying on her stomach, Anna props her chin on her hand. "And what kind of place will it be? Apartment? House?"

"Apartment *and* house," says Eve grandly. "A duplex in New York and a big old mansion in England or something. And an apartment in Paris. Ooh, and a car."

"That's number two," I say, pretending to write it down. "Excellent car."

"New wardrobe . . ." She points at me. "Oh, and I'm going to build you an animal shelter."

"Well, thank you," I say. "But they're kind of expensive."

"I intend to be *extremely* famous," says Eve. Rolling over, she says to Anna, "What do you want?"

Anna looks startled. "Me?"

"Yeah. I've got the houses, the car, and the wardrobe. Syd's got the shelter. We need to get you something."

Anna thinks, says sadly, "I don't know. I don't have a clue what my life is going to be like."

I hurt when Anna says this. She had so much faith in those cards; now she's scared to want anything else in case it doesn't happen. I tell her, "That's because you're good at a lot of things. Eve and I have only one thing we can do, so we're kind of stuck with them."

"No, you guys are just super talented and I'm not," says Anna. "I'm going to be the boring one, always asking about your exciting lives."

"No way," says Eve decisively. "You'll be my manager."

Anna laughs. "Oh, okay."

"Seriously. It's really important when you're famous to keep your old friends. They're the only ones who can tell you when you're full of it."

I grin. "We can do that."

"Yeah?" Suddenly, Eve looks uncertain. "I mean, you will, right? You'll stay my friends?"

Anna says, "What are you, nuts?"

"That falls into the 'duh' category," I tell her.

Anna hugs Eve. "Even if you can be a little impossible at times."

This sends Eve back into fantasyland. As she talks about this house and that concert and that TV special, I suddenly wonder if this was what my dad was like. When he was young, did he imagine that one day he'd be famous and have all these fabulous things? Did he lie on his bed and stare up at the ceiling and think about the success everyone was telling him he would have? Everyone expected my dad would be a famous musician—my dad most of all. But they were wrong.

All of a sudden, I want to yell, *Stop! Forget the houses, forget the cars, forget everyone applauding you. Your mom's right—it might not happen. And you have to be okay if it doesn't. You can't let it wreck you.* Because dreams like that, they can ruin you for real life.

"Oh, hey," says Eve, scrambling for her bag. "I forgot. Guess who sent me a good luck postcard? Mr. Manic Music Man himself—Courtney."

She gets a postcard out of her bag—three, actually—saying, "He sent me one for you guys, too, since I told him you were my 'entourage.' Mine says, 'Dear Ms. Baylor. Good luck. Don't even think of walking out on your obligation to star in my next show! Remember who discovered you!'" She rolls her eyes, but I can tell she's pleased.

I ask Anna, "What's yours say?"

She turns pink as she reads, "'To the only true star I know. Shine bright.'"

It's so goofy, but it's so what Anna needed to hear that I get a little teary. Anna says, "How 'bout yours, Syd?"

Eve says, "He was so crazy about you."

"Pretty crazy, period," I say jokingly. I read, "'Dear Ms. Callender. I truly hope you will choose to explore your musical gifts further at Julliard. Will send info soonest.'"

"Wow," says Anna. "He takes you really seriously. He's never said that to anyone at school."

For a moment I think, *Really? 'Cause that is kind of neat.* Then I shake myself back into reality. "Well, I hate to disappoint him," I say. "But since Eve will be buying me an animal clinic, I don't think I'll have much time for music."

Later I go into the bathroom and dial home to say good night. There's no answer, which is a little weird. Into the machine I say, "Hey, guys, it's me. I'm just wondering how everybody is. Call me."

The next day Eve sings for the screening committee. She comes out waving a red ticket, which means she gets to audition for the actual judges tomorrow. Even though I knew Peter McElroy invited her to audition, I'm still impressed; so many kids have come out with nothing.

I say, "Way to go!"

Eve gives me a strange look. "What'd you think? I wouldn't get in?"

"No, just—it's," I stammer, "that's really cool."

"It's all about the cards, baby," says Eve as she sweeps ahead of us. Anna and I exchange looks. *Baby?*

That night when I call home, my mom picks up, which is awkward because I'm still mad at her for pushing me to leave Beese with Liz. I think maybe she knows that because she sounds stressed, even as she tries to be all up and friendly.

"How's it going? You girls having a blast?"

"Um, sure. How're you guys?"

"Oh . . ." My mom sighs. "Fine. I've hardly been home, Sydney. Work has been, well, the way work always is."

Or the way you always say it is so you don't have to come home, I think. "How's Beese?"

My mom can barely restrain her impatience. "Flourishing, I'm sure."

I wait a moment, then ask, "Is Dad there?"

"No, your father is not here, Sydney." I can tell I've made her angry by asking about Beese and my dad but not really her. But I can't help it. Nothing my mom does or says makes me feel like she thinks of me as someone whose attention is worth having.

"Could you ask him to call me?" I say in a small voice.

"When I see him, I will ask him."

"Thanks," I say. "Well, have a fun time without me." Which sounds weird and not what I meant, but before I can add something, my mom makes kiss noises and hangs up.

In the darkness I fight the "What ifs." What if my

dad's not home because with me out of the house, my parents don't have to pretend they're together? What if he's out of the house so he can drink without my mother seeing? What if he comes home really drunk and she says, *That's it*?

I remember one of my cards: divorce, separation. Supposedly, that's what I was afraid of, not what would happen. But I wonder if you can be so afraid of something that you make it happen?

I look over at Eve, who's snoring on a heap of blankets on the floor. I don't actually believe in God the way some people do, so it feels very strange to pray. I think of it more as talking to the universe. But to the universe or God or whatever, I say, *Please make the cards be right for Eve . . .*

But wrong for me.

SEVEN
TWO OF PENTACLES
Difficulty, inability to launch, embarrassment

The morning of the audition is complete and utter madness. Eve puts clothes on, pulls clothes off. Her mother makes one comment and is immediately banished. Which leaves me and Anna responsible for making sure that Eve doesn't walk out of the hotel butt naked.

Jabbing at Eve's hair with a brush, Anna says, "We have to be out of here in ten minutes."

"But I have to look right!" she wails, kicking shoes across the room and hunting for another pair. "Where're the red ones?"

"I'll find them," I volunteer, searching among the wreckage.

"What about this outfit?" says Anna, holding it up. "It's really cool."

"Yeah—I wore it yesterday!" shrieks Eve.

"So?"

"So? What if one of the judges sees me wearing it both days?"

"They'll think you're poor and feel sorry for you?" I find one of the red shoes and toss it over the bed.

"They'll think I'm a loser. Where's my white skirt?"

I pull it off the lampshade, where it landed when Eve threw it across the room. "Here."

I throw and she catches. Wiggling into it, Eve checks out the results. Then she steps into the red shoes, and says, "What do you think?"

"Perfect!" says Anna, glancing nervously at the clock. Eve looks at me, wanting the truth.

"I think you look totally knockout. But we've got to do something with the hair." Because it looks like a furry pancake right now.

"My spikes!" shrieks Eve, and charges into the bathroom.

Ten minutes later and we're in the car. Eve is yelling at her mom to hurry up. Her mom is reminding her that there is such a thing as speed limits and that if we get arrested, she won't make it to the audition because we will all be in jail. As we tumble out of the car, Eve shouts, "My number!"

"Got it," says Anna, holding up the red piece of paper.

"Uh . . . uh . . ." Eve can't think of anything else she needs. I tug her toward the revolving door. As her mom follows, Eve shrieks, "No!"

"No?" Mrs. Baylor stops.

"No. I just . . . only Anna and Syd."

I feel really sorry for Mrs. Baylor. You can tell: She expected to be there to do the whole jump-and-scream routine when Eve came out of the audition. But I have to hand it to her, she finds a big smile, puts it on her face, and says, "Great. I'll be back in an hour." She gives a wriggling Eve a hug. "Good luck, baby."

"You don't say good luck," says Eve grumpily.

"Then . . . knock 'em dead." She waves as she leaves, but Eve doesn't wave back. As we go in, I remember what Eve said about needing friends who knew you when so they could tell you when you were full of it. Eve may have to be told that soon.

But when I see the hotel ballroom jam-packed with kids and their families, I feel a jolt of sympathy. If I were facing this much competition for something I wanted more than anything, I'd be a stress monster too.

After a long hunt we find three seats together.

A woman in a gray suit comes out with a bullhorn and calls a number: 1421. Eve is 1454. We've got another long wait ahead of us. Anna sits on one side of Eve, I sit on the other. I'm not sure what Eve wants. Total silence? Jokes? Some weird chanting ritual?

Then Anna says, "Hey, I brought you something. A good luck charm." She takes something out of her bag, hands it to Eve. It's a tarot card, the World, the card that was at the end of Eve's reading, promising her fame and fortune and all good things.

Staring down at it, Eve bites her lip.

Anna says, "I think with that and Peter McElroy on your side, you can't go wrong."

"Not to mention your great voice," I put in.

"Not to mention that," Anna agrees.

The door opens. A contestant in a spangle-covered dress comes out. She runs immediately to her mother and bursts into tears. Not "Yay, I made it!" tears. But "They hated me, I'm awful" tears. After a few minutes another contestant walks out. He has a tuba wrapped around his middle and a depressed look on his face. For an hour we watch an endless parade of tears and frustration.

"They're turning everyone down," whispers Eve.

"More room for you, then," I say with more confidence than I feel.

The woman in gray comes out, calls for 1450. At the mention of a number so close to hers, Eve sucks air.

Anna says, "I bet Peter McElroy's already put a note next to your name that says 'Let her through.'"

Eve nods hurriedly. Number 1450 comes out squealing and jumping around in excitement. Her family crowds around her. She's waving a new piece of paper: same number, only this time it's purple.

Eve frowns. I know exactly what she's thinking: Is it a bad sign, someone so close to her in line getting in? Maybe the judges will reject the next ten to show how tough they are.

And this is just one audition in one city, I think. All across the country, kids are waiting, practicing, getting ready to show what they can do. Eve not only has to compete with everyone here, she's competing with all those unseen kids as well.

I am so, so glad it isn't me.

The lady in gray calls, "1451 . . ."

Number 1451 is turned down, as is 1452, a skinny boy with a violin. I don't know why, but I bet he's really good. When he comes out, shaking his head, his dad starts yelling at him. Then he yells at the lady in gray. I feel terrible for the kid. Why do nasty people have children? Why are they allowed to take care of anything?

Then we hear, "1454?" Eve leaps out of her seat.

"Kill 'em," says Anna, squeezing her hand.

"We'll be right here," I tell her.

But Eve barely hears us. Whatever zone performers go into before they do their thing, she's definitely there. As she walks toward the bullhorn lady, she seems unaware of anyone else in the room. I feel a surge of admiration—and maybe a little envy. I wish I could turn off my fear like that. I feel like it's a quality winners have, and while I don't want to be a "winner," I don't want to be a loser, either. Which is what I feel like when I let fear take over. Fingering my cell phone in my pocket, I tell myself for the thousandth time that everything is fine at home.

I hear Anna ask, "Do you think she'll get picked?"

"Do you?"

Anna hesitates, then says firmly, "Yes."

"I think so too."

"Here's the other question, though."

"What?"

"Can we deal with her if she does?"

I burst out laughing. "Excellent question!"

We wait. Maybe I'm nuts, but I think Eve has been in there longer than Tuba Kid or Spangle Girl. They weren't picked, so that's a good sign, isn't it?

Anna breathes, "I can't stand this."

"I know."

Then Anna says, "You know, I haven't wanted to say it. But ever since my reading didn't come true . . ."

Before she can finish, the door opens. Anna and I jump up, ready to collide with a gleeful, shrieking Eve. But something's wrong. Eve's not jumping. Or shrieking. In fact, she seems to be barely moving. Glancing at Anna, I hurry over to her. As we approach, she seems to wake up. Barging past us, she snarls, "Don't. Speak. Don't. Say. Anything."

I look at her hands. No purple card. Oh, my God. She didn't make it.

I start, "No way . . ."

"No," she says. "Really. Another word, and I'll kill someone."

Not knowing what to do, Anna and I follow her out of the hotel. When we see her mother at the revolving doors, Anna waves her hands like, *Warning: Thunderstorms!* But Mrs. Baylor is focused on Eve. Arms open, she says brightly, "How'd it go?"

Eve yells, "Get away from me! This is all your fault!" Then she shoves past her and out onto the street.

For blocks we walk ten feet behind Eve so we don't freak her out. I feel beyond horrible. I killed Eve's dream by hoping the cards were wrong. I don't know how, but all my negativity must have nudged the universe. Either that or the cards were just a cruel joke all along . . . but God, I wish they weren't.

At one point I call out, "Eve, let's just go back to the hotel."

Anna adds, "We'll order room service . . ."

"Watch any dumb movie you want . . ."

Eve doesn't answer. But at the next corner she swerves in the direction of the hotel. She bangs through the doors and stalks down the carpet, not caring if she bumps into guests or bellboys or luggage. We follow, apologizing to anyone and everyone.

No one says a word in the elevator. When we get out, Eve heads straight toward our room. Anna follows, glancing back at me and Mrs. Baylor, who says, "Eve, honey . . ."

"No!" Eve shouts, not even looking back.

Watching her go, Mrs. Baylor sighs. "I guess I'm the last person she wants to see right now."

I say, "I don't think she wants people to see her right now. You know, why would anyone want to if she's not going to be on TV?"

Mrs. Baylor shakes her head. "I never should have let her try out for this."

"I don't think you could have stopped her."

She smiles. "Let me know when a mother's touch is needed, okay? I've got to go back and get the car from the hotel parking lot."

I smile back, happy I've made at least one person feel better. "Sure thing."

I go back to our room to find Anna standing by the bathroom door. No sign of Eve. I worry that she's disappeared until Anna scribbles on a piece of paper—*She's locked herself in*—and points to the bathroom.

Pulling her over by the window, I whisper, "You don't think she's going to do anything crazy, do you?"

Anna raises an eyebrow. "Eve?"

She's right. We rush to the door, pound on it. Anna calls, "Eve?"

There's no answer. Worried, she looks at me.

I say, "Eve, they're idiots. It doesn't matter."

There's a pause. Then, through the door, we hear, "You didn't think they were idiots when they liked me."

"What did they say?" asks Anna.

A howl: "They didn't pick me, okay! Who cares what they said?"

Then we hear a thud. I shout, "Eve, are you okay?"

There's no answer. "Eve!"

Anna rattles the doorknob. It turns immediately and the door opens. We peer in and see Eve in the bathtub, which is full. Which is odd because she's wearing all her clothes. Including her red shoes. Well, one of them. The other got thrown across the room. That was the thud.

After a long pause Anna says, "Taking a bath and washing your clothes at the same time. Cool idea."

"I bet it catches on," I say. "Saves water."

"And time," says Anna.

"Shut up," says Eve, sinking her chin lower in the water. Her hair is all wet. At the other end of the tub her feet are sticking out. One red shoe. One bare foot, with five pink toes, painted with green nail polish. Her mascara's run, and she looks like a seriously pissed-off panda.

There's something so sad and so funny about the sight of Eve in the bath, something that makes me so glad she's my friend that I smile. Then grin. And—it's the worst, but I can't help it—I get a fit of the giggles.

Anna stares at me horrified. Clamping my hand to my mouth, I say, "I'm sorry."

Eve is outraged. "Hello—miserable, crushed person here!"

"I know, I know, I'm sorry . . ." I sit down on the toilet, turn my face to the wall, thinking if I can't see Eve, the laughter will stop.

But it doesn't work. Anna and Eve gaze at me, totally confused, and that makes me giggle again. Then Eve disappears under the water in a huff, and I lose it completely. I fall off the toilet, I'm laughing so hard. Poor Anna doesn't know whether to help me or stop Eve from drowning.

I gasp, "It's just . . . it's just . . ." Eve surfaces, spraying water everywhere. Anna throws towels over the floor to soak it up. "It's just they were so *dumb* not to pick you. If they could see you now, they'd be kicking themselves. Who would not want to watch you?"

A smile quirks the side of Eve's mouth. "Well, that's what I thought, definitely."

"I mean . . ." I almost have control back when I spot Eve's shoe on the floor. That sends me off again. After a few seconds Anna starts laughing too. Finally, even Eve starts to giggle.

Then Mrs. Baylor appears at the door. For a moment we all stop laughing; the bathroom is a disaster area. She says, "What in the world happened?"

We collapse in hysterical laughter.

After we clean up the bathroom—Mrs. Baylor orders up extra towels and a mop from the hotel—Mrs. Baylor declares that we are going out to dinner to celebrate.

"Celebrate what?" sniffs Eve.

"The fact that you're still a free artist, unchained by gross commercial interests," says Mrs. Baylor lightly. "Come on, star. Let's get ready."

When they're gone, Anna goes to take a shower while I tidy up the bedroom. I know the maids do it, but it seems rude to leave them a big mess. When the phone rings, I jump on it. Finally—my dad.

But when I pick up, the voice isn't my dad's. And it says, "Hi, Mom."

I say, "Uh, I think you have the wrong number."

"Oh, sorry . . . wait, is this Syd?"

Confused, I say, "Yes."

"It's Mark."

"Oh!" I guess they put him through to the wrong room. "How are you?"

"Uh, good. So, how was the big audition?"

I hesitate. "Well, you didn't hear it from me, but she didn't make it."

"Good," he says firmly.

"Good?" *Is* Mark jealous of Eve?

"Yeah. If she got on that show, they'd try to turn her into Muzak. And that would suck."

I want to tell Mark that it is unfair for him to say wonderful things when I am trying to get over my crush on him. People should not be outrageously perfect and not love you back. Or if they are, they should at least not flaunt how amazing they are. It's annoying.

Then he says, "I bet she's taking it well."

"Only one bathroom destroyed."

He laughs. "Well, it's a good thing you're there. If it was just my mom, the whole hotel would be at risk."

I should point out that Anna is also here. That it's not just me calming Eve down. But I can't. Every time Mark says "you," it proves he is aware of me, and I feel a surge of happiness. I'm like a junkie, hopelessly hooked on any sign that he might see me as something other than his sister's goofy friend.

On impulse, I say, "My dad's a musician. He gets intense too. So I guess Eve makes sense to me."

"Oh," he says, and for a second I kick myself for babbling. Then he asks, "So do you do anything musical?"

"Piano. I . . . play," I add lamely.

"Are you good?"

"No. I mean . . . I don't know. I love it, I don't think about 'good.'"

"No," says Mark. "It's like when people say, 'Oh, you really know computers.'" I cringe, wondering if he remembers I'm one of those people. "I think, 'Well, you would be too if you spent twenty out of every twenty-four hours on one."

I laugh. "You don't."

"Maybe you've noticed, my family is a little . . . dramatic."

I hesitate, then admit, "Yeah."

"But with the computer, it's all there on the screen. It's the whole world, but different."

"Like music. When I'm playing really well—which is not that often, believe me—I feel like I'm feeling everything that's possible, all this emotion, but . . ."

"It's not screaming."

"Right."

There's a long pause. Something has happened, but I'm not sure what. Insanely, I'm about to say, *When I get back, do you want to . . . ?* when Mark says, "So . . . is my mom there?"

And all I can say is, "Sure, I'll get her."

EIGHT
NINE OF WANDS, UPSIDE DOWN
Adversity, ill health

Mrs. Baylor takes us out to a really nice restaurant, the kind of place where you expect to see someone famous any minute. Eve is either in a better mood or putting up a great front. She refuses to say what happened during the audition, and no one wants to push her. Instead, she does hilarious imitations of the kids who did make it. I laugh harder than anyone because I still feel so guilty. Logically, I know I didn't wreck Eve's audition—but the fact that even a small part of me wanted my friend not to get what she wants most in the world makes me feel awful.

And now I have another reason to feel terrible. Forget cures, forget embarrassment. I am massively in love with Mark Baylor and I don't know what to do about it. Before, it was just a crush, an "Oh, God, he's so cool" thing. My big daydream was that someday he might talk to me.

Now he has talked to me—twice—and it's awful. Or great—I can't decide. Great because, despite the fact that he's more than two years older than me, I'm starting to think he might like me. Awful because, even if he does, Eve would go bananas.

As the waiter takes away our appetizer plates, Anna nudges me, saying, "I have to go to the bathroom, want to come?"

Puzzled, I follow her to the ladies' room, which is beautiful like the rest of the restaurant. The lights change color, from red to orange to blue. At the sink the water flows out of the wall like a waterfall. Washing her hands, Anna says, "Are you okay?"

Surprised, I lie, "Yeah. Why?"

"You're silent. Are you worried about Beesley?"

"Yeah, I . . ." I falter. All the thoughts about Mark that have been crowding my head for the last hour turn into words and start tumbling out of my mouth. "No, actually. I mean, yes. But I have another problem."

Her eyes widen. "What?"

"I . . ." I hesitate because this is going to sound so pitiful. "I like someone I really shouldn't like."

Anna's surprise turns to smiles. "Cool! Who?"

"You cannot tell. I'm serious."

"Yeah, right, who would I tell? Eve, but—"

"You especially can't tell Eve."

Anna goes still. "Why not?"

"Because . . . the someone that I'm not supposed to like is her brother."

I wait for the laugh. For *Mark Baylor? The mega geek? Are you serious?* But there is no laugh. Instead, Anna says, "Oh. My. God." So she understands the direness of the situation.

"Yeah."

"Does he—wait, nothing's happened, has it?"

"Um, no. But also yes?"

"Oh, my God." Anna leans against the sink.

"I mean nothing . . . nothing . . . I don't know if he likes me or not. But I always assumed totally not, and now I think maybe, maybe he does. And if he does, I have to do something about it, but I don't know what. Will you help me?"

"*Me?* Hello, romantic disaster area over here."

"You're the only one I know who's actually had"—I bring myself up short—"has a boyfriend."

"Had," Anna corrects me. She stares helplessly at the toilet stall. "Eve will go nuclear."

"I know—but I can't think about that right now. It

143

probably won't happen, but I feel like I'll go crazy if I don't at least find out if Mark likes me."

"What do you want me to help you with?"

"Just . . . how to find out if a guy likes you. And what to do if he does."

"Eve can *never* know," says Anna.

"No, I'll never tell her."

Biting her lip, she thinks. "Okay, first question. When he sees you—"

At that moment the door swings open and Eve barges in. "Here you are! I was like, Did they drown in the toilet or something?"

I swallow, feeling guilty. "Nope, just . . . yakking."

"Oh?" Eve looks suspiciously at each of us. Part of the problem of being best friends with two people is that what one knows, the other has to know—otherwise, they feel left out. And this is something Eve can't know, at least not yet.

"I was moaning about Nelson," says Anna. "I figured you and your mom wouldn't want to hear it."

For a second it seems like Eve will say, *Yeah, you got that right.* But instead, she hugs Anna and says, "Hey, it's like *Making It!* If they don't want you, they're losers, and that goes double for Nelson. Okay?"

Anna smiles. "Okay."

"Can we go? My fries will get cold."

The next morning we drive home. The closer we get to the city, the quieter Eve gets. As she stares out the window, she's probably remembering her big promises, how she told the doormen they could be her bodyguards. Now she has to go back and say, *Oops! Didn't quite make it on* Making It!

At one point she says, "I don't know. Maybe I picked the wrong song."

"What do you mean?" I ask her.

She just shrugs. But a few minutes later she bursts out with, "I don't understand how the cards . . ."

"The cards were never real," I say gently. "They were a game, something fun. We all took them too seriously."

Upset, Eve stares at me, wanting to argue. But what can she say? She goes back to staring out the window.

Before we go into the tunnel, I try calling my house. I know I'm being silly; we're so close to home now. But I'll just feel better if I hear my dad say, *Hey, everything's fine. Quit worrying.*

Amazingly, my dad picks up on the second ring. I say, "Dad! Hey, it's me."

"Syd." For a moment it seems like that's all he'll say. Then, "How was it?"

"Oh . . ." I glance at Eve, who's tearing at her nails with her teeth. "It was a scene. How're you?"

"Okay," says my dad. "We missed you."

"Yeah, I missed you."

Something's off, I can feel it. "How's Beese?"

A long, ugly pause. "You'll see when you get home," says my dad.

"What do you mean?" My voice rises, and Anna looks at me, worried.

"Well, honey. You'll see."

"Dad—tell me."

"He's not doing so great, baby, but we'll call Liz when you get back and—"

Call Liz when I get back? Why haven't they called Liz already? "Call her now, Dad. Is he throwing up? Not eating, what?" I want to tell Mrs. Baylor to stop the car so I can run all the way home.

"We'll talk when you get here, sweetie."

"No, Dad . . ." But Mrs. Baylor is entering the tunnel. All of a sudden, the light goes, we're swallowed by concrete, and the connection is gone.

I barely say good-bye to Eve or thank Mrs. Baylor. I only half hear Anna yell "Call me!" as I jump out of the car. As I drag my bag through the lobby to the elevator, I think I should have left the stupid thing.

It's slowing me down, and I have to get to Beesley.

As the elevator crawls to my floor, I'm thinking that maybe it's not so bad. Maybe my dad is freaking out because Beese is a little sick and I left him in charge. Maybe I'll see him and go, *Oh, you're fine, please don't scare me like that.* Or, no, I won't say that. If Beesley is fine, I'll be the nicest, sweetest, noncomplainingest . . .

But the moment I see Beese, lying on his favorite blanket in my room, I know he's not fine. He doesn't move as I come in. He barely opens his eyes. He's in a strange position, and after a few seconds I realize that he's in pain. He's been in pain all this time and no one has helped him. He's lain here with no Liz, no me . . .

How could I have done this? How could I have left him?

I look back at my dad, who's standing by the door. "When did he get like this?"

My dad shifts from one foot to the other. "Sometime after you left."

Which doesn't tell me much, but right now it's more important to call Liz than to grill my dad. As the phone rings, I pray, *Please be there, please be there, please be there,* and I wonder if that's what Beese has been thinking about me all this time.

I will make you better, Beese, I promise him. *I'm getting you help right now.*

As I wait for Liz to pick up, I ask my dad, "When was the last time he had his medication?"

"A little while."

"Like, how long?" But then Rosie, Liz's assistant, answers and I say, "Hello, Rosie? It's Syd. Is Liz around? I . . . kind of have an emergency."

An hour later Liz is examining Beesley. She gently presses his stomach, which causes him to shut his eyes tight, then says to my dad, "When did he last eat?"

"It's been a day or two," my dad says.

I look at him. "I said to call if he wasn't eating."

"I kept hoping he'd get hungry, sweetheart."

Liz strokes Beesley's back. "And the meds, was he okay with them?"

"Not really."

Liz looks at Beese's eyes. Echoes, "Not really."

"It was a struggle, getting them down."

"So . . . he hasn't had them in a while." Liz's voice is totally calm, just the facts.

"That's about right," says my dad.

"Like . . . since I left?" I guess.

"I gave them right after you left. But even then, he was resisting me, baby. I'm . . . not sure how much got down his throat."

I go cold. Beese has to have his meds twice a day. If he misses even a day, it's really bad news for his

148

kidneys. What my dad is telling me is that he hasn't had his meds since I left. He's been off them for three whole days.

Is he going to die? That's what I want to ask Liz. But only so she can say, *Don't be silly, of course not.* And you shouldn't ask questions when you can stand to hear only one answer.

Liz stands up, says to my dad, "Can I have a moment with Sydney?"

Here is what Liz tells me in that moment. She tells me Beesley's kidneys have shut down. She tells me he is in pain. She tells me there are things she could do to prolong his life. But they are not easy, and Beesley is not young.

Sometimes you cry because you think of something and make yourself sad. Other times it's like bleeding—a part of you is torn and you're not even aware emotion is flowing out of you. Except that it hurts. It really, really, hurts.

"What would you do?" I ask her. "If he were yours?"

"He's not mine, honey."

"But if he were." Because I know Liz would stop at nothing to save an animal she loved. But I also know there's no way she'd put that animal through pain. "I won't be mad if it's different from what I'd do. I just want to know what you truly think."

Liz looks at Beesley. In a tight voice she says, "I'd let him go, sweetie."

Somehow it's not the thought that Beesley is at the end of his life that destroys me, it's the idea that he is in such pain, his life isn't worth living. Because I did that to him by leaving him with someone I should never have trusted.

"He wouldn't be this sick if my dad had given him the medication, would he?" It's my second impossible question to Liz, and for a moment I'm scared she won't answer.

"He would have eventually gotten to this point," says Liz carefully.

"But not this quick. Not this bad."

"No."

"Okay," I say. "Okay."

"Okay what, sweetie?" Liz asks gently.

"All of it. What you said. Okay."

Liz gives Beesley something for the pain. Tomorrow she will come back, and it will happen. At first I think, *Oh, she doesn't have whatever she needs with her.* Then I realize, *She's giving me time to say good-bye.*

But I don't know how to say good-bye. I want to ask

150

Anna and Eve to come over so I don't have to be alone with this. But because I left Beese to be with them, it seems wrong to have them here. As for Tat and Mouli, animals don't always like being around sick animals, and I don't want any ugliness to touch Beese now.

When my mom comes home, she asks, "Can I do anything?" I shake my head. "You hungry at all? I could bring you dinner in here—that way, you can stay with him."

My throat goes tight. "Thanks." As my mom turns to leave, I say, "Mom?"

"Yes, baby?"

"What happened?" She looks uncomfortable. "Something was going on when I called."

She sighs. "Let's talk about this later, sweetie."

"No, now. I want to know."

So she tells me. There've been complaints from the students in the gifted class. About my dad. They said he's been showing up late. Smelling of alcohol. They said he rants about nothing half the time. And lately, he's stuck earphones in his ears and listened to music all class.

While I was away, he fell asleep in class, and the kids called the janitor. Who found a bottle in my dad's desk drawer.

"So," says my mom tiredly, "I think that's it for

that job." Then she shakes herself, says, "Don't think about this now, sweetheart. You be with Beesley."

So I am. I play his favorite Beatles album, *Abbey Road*. I tell him about my trip, talk about Mrs. Rosemont, make up stories about his life on the street. I want to be cheerful, not all weepy. No anxiety for Beese now.

But as I do all this, I'm thinking that my dad didn't forget about Beese because of his job. He forgot about Beese because he was drunk. He promised and he lied. No wonder I never found any bottles at home. He was keeping them at work. Why didn't I think of that?

Because I didn't want to. I was like my dad, plugging happy thoughts in my ears, blocking out everything else. My mom warned me. She said I should leave Beese with Liz. She knew. I didn't listen. The same way I didn't listen to the cards. I cringe now when I remember telling Eve they were just a game, that we took them too seriously. I thought I could fight them, prove them wrong. But they proved me wrong in the worst way.

At some point there's a knock on the door. I tell myself, *No one's there. Don't answer.*

After a while no one goes away.

I will never think of my dad as a person again. I don't know what he is now. But he's not the person I decided he was when I was five years old or whatever.

152

I don't even know if he ever was that person or if we just need to think our parents are nice people. It doesn't matter. Something has just gone completely dead inside. It's a useful thing, probably something the body does for self-protection. Shuts down the reactor neurons to things that are dangerous.

I test this. I pull up memories: How my dad took me to my first concert. How he helped me with math and told me that even if I didn't like it, I couldn't be afraid of it. How he knows that certain people are ridiculous.

I feel nothing. Think: *Good.*

The next day I start to cry when I see Liz at the door. Her face creases up too, and she reaches out and squeezes my arm. "I know," she says. "I know."

Then she says, "There's no rule we have to do this today, you know."

I shake my head. "No. He's not happy. I don't . . . I don't . . ." I want to say, *I don't want him to be in pain anymore,* but I can't get the words out.

Beesley is lying in a nest of blankets. He doesn't even look up as Liz comes in.

When Widget died, my parents didn't let me be with him. Just had Liz do it in her office. They took him and I never saw him again. I always hated that. That he was alone when he died. I don't want that for Beesley. He's been abandoned so many times in his life—first on the street, then when Mrs. Rosemont died. I want him to know he's loved at the end. That he's leaving his home, people who will miss him.

"Do you want to hold him?" Liz asks.

I nod. Carefully lift Beesley up in the blankets and settle him on my lap. I don't want him to feel how upset I am, so I try to keep my voice normal as I stroke his head. "You're going to feel better, Beesley. You're not going to be tired and in pain anymore. Liz is going to make you better. . . ."

But that's a lie. She's not going to make him better. She's going to end his life.

I hope it was a good life, Beesley, I think. *I hope you had the warmest, safest, most love-filled life, because you deserved it. I hope you know how much Mrs. Rosemont loved you. How much I love you. . . .*

I choke out, "I don't want him to go."

I feel Liz's hand on my head. "I know. But it's not up to us." I nod because I know this. Hug Beesley closer.

After a moment Liz says, "Ready?" I nod again.

There are two needles. The first one makes Beesley sleep, so he doesn't feel a thing. The second stops his heart. I hold him, whisper in his ear, ". . . the best cat, Beesley. The best cat, the sweetest, most gentle . . ."

With the first needle, Beesley relaxes. All the stiff-ness of pain melts away. For a split second I think, *We could just do this.*

But we can't, and the second needle goes in. And I feel it—as Beesley dies, I feel him leave. His body goes limp, feels lighter, emptied of his spirit. And he just isn't there anymore. There's a body. But no Beesley. People always say, "Oh, I can't believe so-and-so is dead." But if you hold someone? You know what death is.

I can't stand it, the emptiness. It's horrible. As I fold the blanket over Beesley so Liz can take him, I think there shouldn't be bodies without life in them. It's wrong. And yet it's reality, for everyone. Like Liz said, *It's not up to us.*

Except this time it was up to us. I know Beesley didn't have a lot of time left, but my dad took even that little bit of time away from him. And it's because of me—because I was stupid and a baby and trusted him—that my dad had that power. The cards said there would be death, and there was. But there didn't have to be. It wasn't fated to be—I just screwed up.

But maybe that's what fate is, one human screwup after another.

NINE

TEN OF WANDS

Intrigue, deceiver, a traitor

Afterward, I call Eve and Anna. As I dial Eve's number, I'm nervous. She's dealing with her own misery right now. Plus, she can get sarcastic when you're feeling vulnerable. It's like she's not comfortable with it, so she needs to make fun.

But when I tell her Beesley died, she goes completely quiet. Finally, she says, "Were you there?"

"Uh-huh."

"Was it weird? Like, when he was gone?"

Which is sort of the absolute wrong question but also the right one. "Yeah, it was. They're really . . . gone, you know?"

"I've never seen anything dead."

"Me neither. But I'm glad. That I was with him."

There's a long pause. Then Eve says, "I don't know if I could handle it. You know, if it were Tat."

One day, I think, *it will be.* "Why don't you go give her a hug? In memory of Beese?"

"Yeah," says Eve. "I think I will. Hey—"

"Yeah?"

"Beese didn't die 'cause you came with me to the audition? Like, if you'd been here . . ."

I can hear the anxiety in her voice, the fear that it's her fault. But it's not her fault, and I tell her so.

Anna starts crying the second I tell her. She took care of Beesley for Mrs. Rosemont, so she knew him even before I did. I say, "I know. It really sucks."

"What happened?"

My throat goes tight. I can't tell her about my dad right now. "He just . . . got worse."

"The house must feel so empty."

I look around my room. Beesley's crate and blanket are still on the floor. It feels wrong to get rid of them. "Yeah." I choke up. "Look—I'm sorry I didn't call you guys. I thought of Mouli and Tat saying good-bye, but . . ."

"No, I understand. We could do something now, though, if you want."

"Like a funeral?" I hadn't thought of this, but it

makes sense. Beesley had friends, cat friends and human friends. They deserve a chance to say good-bye. "Liz is going to give me his ashes. We could scatter them someplace he loved."

Only—what place did Beesley love? He was a stray; for a long time he had no home. There's Mrs. Rosemont's apartment, but I don't think the new owners would be thrilled about having kitty ashes scattered all over the place. There's my place, but the thought of keeping him resting in peace in a box on my shelf is weird—not to mention slightly gross.

Then I remember what it felt like when he died, that sense that the Beesleyness of Beesley had floated out of his body, like a scent or a breeze. Where did it go? I can't picture Beesley on a cloud somewhere in Cat Heaven. I like to think of him as still here somehow. Essence du Beesley, floating in the ether, making the world a little nicer, a little more civilized.

"I know what we can do," I say.

The next day Anna, Eve, and I meet at my house. Eve brings Tat. Anna has Mouli. I bring Beesley's ashes.

Anna says, "Ready?"

As I'll ever be, I think, and nod. The three of us troop up to the roof of our building. As we shove open the door and walk out into the bright sunlight,

I know I picked the perfect place. Our building is high—looking around, you mostly see sky. Only in the distance do you see the rest of the city. Rooftops and streets, water towers, cars, tiny people bustling about. For a moment I worry that Beesley wouldn't want to be a part of all that noise, that the country and quiet would be better for him. I thought of the park, but I didn't want dogs peeing on him.

But, really, he was a city cat, so this feels right.

Anna sets Mouli's crate down. Eve, I notice, isn't letting go of Tat.

"Where do you want to do it?" asks Anna.

I point to the lowest wall. "There seems good."

It's a breezy day, and fortunately, the wind is blowing in the right direction. As Eve jokes, you wouldn't want a face full of Beesley.

What Liz gave me is a pretty tin, white with green flowers on it. It's surprisingly heavy. I open it. For a moment I stare at the pile of ash. This is it? All that's left of all that life and sweetness and love?

I squeeze back tears, think, *Good-bye, Beesley*. Then ask, "Anyone want to say anything?"

There's a moment of silence; no one wants to be first or weird or dorky. Then Eve says, "Bye, Beesley. Tat says ciao."

Anna's mouth is tight; she's trying not to lose it. In

a small voice she says, "Say hi to Mrs. Rosemont."

"Oh, yeah," I say to the box. "You'll see Mrs. Rosemont—that's kind of cool." Then, when no one says anything else, I say, "Okay?"

"Okay," says Eve. Anna nods.

Holding the box over the ledge, I let Beesley's ashes stream out. They're gray—just like his soulful eyes. As they float out into the air, I say, "Bye, Beesley! Thank you!"

I don't know what I'm thanking him for. I guess, just for being.

Anna drops off Mouli at her place, and we go over to Eve's house. Anna's mom has friends over, and I don't want to be anywhere near my dad.

At Eve's we settle on the floor in her room. Propped against the bed, Anna clasps her hands in her lap. "So, I have this question, but I'm not sure I should ask."

She looks to me and I say, "Go ahead."

"Remember the reading? How it said someone would die?"

I feel myself freeze up. "A little hard to forget, yeah."

"Just . . . maybe this was the Death card, you know? Maybe it meant Beesley's death, not your . . . Maybe it had nothing to do with your dad, is what I'm saying."

I've thought the same thing. But if that's true, it's just more proof of how cruel the cards can be. Beesley didn't deserve to die, whereas my dad is so lost in how miserable he is, he can't even take care of things he's supposed to.

If Anna thinks the cards are doing me a favor killing Beesley, I'm not in the mood to appreciate it. All the sadness I've been feeling sours, turns ugly. I feel sharp and impatient. Let's get real. The cards didn't kill Beesley—my dad did. I did.

"I don't want to talk about the stupid cards," I say.

Anna and Eve glance at each other. Eve says, "You have to admit, it's a little eerie."

I say, "Here's what's eerie to me: You guys still believe this garbage has any meaning. Like there's some divine plan, and if you do the right thing, it all works out okay. Anna, you were supposed to get love. Well, no Declan and no Nelson. So much for that."

Eve opens her mouth, so I turn on her. "And you got the fame and fortune you wanted, right? Cards really came through for you there."

I know I'm being mean. But I don't care. Crazily, I feel like Anna and Eve talked me into doing this reading. It was an unspoken rule: We all got cats, we all had to do a reading. Well, I did my reading, and it's brought me nothing but pain. And if Anna and Eve want to pretend it's done anything good for them, fine, but I'm not buying into it and I wish they'd shut up about it.

Stroking Tat, Eve says, "I still think it's going to happen for me." But her voice is uncertain.

"Right," says Anna. "And . . . I don't know what's going to happen with Nelson, but I feel like the cards got my situation right."

"Because you want to believe it," I say, exasperated. "Because you both got happy readings. Well, yay, but some of us didn't."

I hate how I sound right now, snotty and mean and woe is me. But they're driving me nuts with their faith. It's like they're in this little club of "I believe" and anyone who doesn't agree is just pathetic.

"But the bad part of your reading doesn't have to come true," says Eve. "You can do things—"

"To change it, I know. What I do, how I act, affects the future. Oops, guess I shouldn't have gone with you to Philadelphia, because if I hadn't, Beesley would be alive right now. Right?"

Eve drops her head, unable to look at me. Nastily, I say again, "Right?"

When no one says anything, I say, "Whatever . . . ," and get up. As I slam Eve's door behind me, I hear Anna call my name, but I'm not stopping. At this moment I hate them both. I hate them for being so trusting, so certain that the world is nice and everything's going to work out just fine.

I so need to be out of here. Unfortunately, Eve's front door has a hundred stupid locks on it. Turn this way, pull that, undo chain . . . every time I turn the knob, something else needs opening. Frustrated, I turn knobs back and forth, start rattling the handle. I'm about to kick the door when I hear, "Wait, wait, stop."

A hand comes over my shoulder, undoes all the locks.

"There," says Mark. "Now try it."

Helplessly, I say, "Sorry."

"No problem. Just didn't want you to break the door." He peers at my face. "Did Eve go psycho on you?"

"No! No. Just, you know . . . my cat died." My voice dries up completely on the word "died."

"Oh." Mark nods once. "I *didn't* know, actually."

Of course Eve wouldn't have told him; she always keeps friends and family separate. I'm sure Mark doesn't care about a cat, so I say, "He was old," so he doesn't feel he has to burst into tears.

"Still," says Mark carefully, "he was your cat. And cats are . . . important. Look, come and have a soda or something. Eve'll chill and come out and say how sorry she is. Well, not that she's sorry—actually, it was all your fault and you were a jerk . . ." I laugh, because that is exactly how Eve "apologizes." ". . . but since you're lucky to have her in your miserable life, you might as well make up."

Sitting down at the table, I say, "I don't think she's ever said that. That I have a miserable life." *She'd be right*, I think, *but she's never said it.*

Mark sits down opposite me. "Actually, her life is pretty miserable these days. She's still bummed about that stupid audition."

"She really thought it was going to happen for her." Mark hands me a can of soda. I sip it only to have something to do with my hands.

"It can still happen," he says. "It's not like her life is over because of this one thing."

I know what Eve is feeling. Some things feel so huge that when they happen or don't happen, it *is* like your life's over. And in a way, it's true—the life you had, the person you were . . . that is over. You're never going back.

"Tell me about your cat," says Mark. "You must have been really nuts about him."

"Well . . . yeah," I say, echoing Mark's careful tone. "You get kind of nuts about your pets."

"I wouldn't know. I had a turtle when I was six. It was dead for a week before my parents noticed. I kept saying, 'He's not moving,' and they were like, 'He's a turtle, what do you want?'"

"That's awful. Were you sad?"

"Not really. My grandmother Yvonne got him for me because she wanted me to connect with something living. So it was kind of a forced thing."

I smile. "My mom always wants me to connect with people instead of animals."

"Yeah, my parents have given up on the people thing."

He says it so seriously, I laugh. "Why?"

"Because I'm not interested in people. I think they're pretty horrible."

"Me too!" I sit up. "Well, not all people. I mean, I actually *like* most people. But they freak me out. In a way animals don't. Which is sad on my part, let's face it."

"No," says Mark. "Wise. Is that why you're so upset about your cat?"

"No." I take a deep breath. "The reason I'm upset is that . . . Okay, I'm always saying people freak me out, you can't trust them, blah-blah-blah." I swallow. "When the fact is, Beesley trusted me, and he shouldn't have. I let him down."

"How?"

"I let him die. I left him with someone I knew wouldn't take care of him—well, I should have known this person wouldn't take care of him. And he didn't. So Beese didn't get the medicine he was supposed to, and he died." My throat is aching. I dig my hands into my eyes. If Mark can't deal with humans, a crying girl has to be tops on his list of nightmares.

Mark is quiet for a long moment. "Why did you think you could trust this person?"

"Because it was my dad, and he said he'd do it. But I should've known."

"A dad sounds pretty safe to me."

"Well, he's not." Mark raises his eyebrows in a question. "My dad's a mess, and I don't know what to do about it."

I glance at Mark to see how horrified he is. His face is a total blank. Shrugging, I say, "I know—pathetic. Sorry. I don't mean to . . ." I get up from the table. "I'm just going to go now."

Blindly, I look for Beesley's ash box. It's here somewhere—I put it down when I came in. But of course I can't find it now. For a second I think of leaving it behind, getting it later. But I can't leave Beesley behind again. I can't . . .

Then I feel a hand on my arm, hear Mark say, "Okay, um, stop."

Desperate, I say, "Really, I'll get out of your way."

"You don't..." The grip on my arm tightens. "Stop, seriously. I don't want you to leave."

This is so ridiculous, I laugh. "Um, I'm pretty sure that you do."

Then I realize the hand isn't gripping my arm anymore; it's rubbing it. Or patting it—I can't tell. Sort of both. I look up at Mark. He's frowning. Then he heaves a big sigh like, *God, might as well . . .* and kisses me.

I have never been kissed before, and at first all I can think is, *Oh, my God, kissing.* Then it occurs to me that I can't just stand here—kissing's a two-way street, I have to kiss back. So I do. At least I try. But how can you tell the difference between moving your mouth around and kissing?

After a few seconds I get it. There is a big, big difference.

Then I hear, "Get off of her, you perv!"

I jerk my head away, see Eve standing at the entrance to the kitchen. Mark yells, "Get out of here, will you?"

"I will not get out of here!" Eve storms into the kitchen, yanks me away. "You're a pig. Her cat just *died* and you're jumping on her? That's low, Mark, really, really low."

I stammer, "Eve, he—he didn't jump on me."

"Don't stick up for him, Syd." She glares at Mark. "This is so wrong."

Frustrated, I say, "It's not wrong, Eve. It's . . . great. Okay?"

Just then Anna comes into the kitchen. She takes one look at all of us and says, "Uh-oh."

Eve turns on her. "Uh-oh? Wait a minute, you knew about this?"

Anna panics. "Um, no. I mean . . ." She shoots me a "Help!" look.

Mark says, "Eve, quit with the drama. It's none of your business."

"Oh, no." Eve waves a finger in the air. "No, no, no. It is so my business. You know why? Because this is incest." She points to me. "We are sisters. He is my brother. Which makes him your brother. Which makes this beyond gross. Okay?"

Anna says, "I don't think it's the same thing . . ."

"Don't you even try to stick up for them!" Eve yells. "Don't you even—!" She glares at me. "God, how could you? What, is this why you hang out with me? Because you're hot for Major Anal Nerd? I mean, now I get it. How stupid was I? Thinking we were friends. I should have understood: It was about *lo-ove*." She whines the word "love." "God, make me sick."

"Eve, come on, we've been friends for forever."

"Yeah, well, maybe you've liked him for forever, how do I know?"

What I need to say here is, *I have not liked Mark for forever!* But I'm so confused, with Eve yelling at me and Mark kissing me, I'm not sure. Have I? What I know for a fact is that I'm not friends with Eve just because of Mark. We've been friends since we were nine, for God's sake.

Except . . . except . . . Eve was Anna's friend first. And I was Anna's friend first. And, really, it's only because of Anna that we became friends. That's something I haven't thought about in a long time.

"Look"—Eve folds her arms—"we'll make this really simple. Choose. Me or Mark. If you're really my friend, this is an easy choice."

"It's a dumb choice," Mark breaks in.

"Eve, come on . . . ," says Anna.

I tell myself Eve is only doing this because she's still upset over not getting picked for *Making It!* That she always has to feel chosen and that Mark is one of the major reasons for that—not that it's his fault, but their parents always make more of a fuss over him than they do over Eve. I tell myself I have to be nice here.

But I'm sick of being nice. And I'm sick of Eve feeling oppressed and sorry for herself. If their parents like Mark more than her, maybe it's because Mark isn't a pain in the butt and she is.

I say, "I'm not making that choice, Eve."

Her eyes narrow. "Really."

"Yes, really."

"Hmm—well, that's interesting, because you in fact did make the choice. By not making it. Guess what? You chose Mark. So . . . fine. Have a nice life. And while you're at it? Get out of my house, you traitor."

Then she turns around and marches back to her room.

TEN

TWO OF CUPS, UPSIDE DOWN

False friendship, crossed desires, separation

All the way home, I am furious at Eve. What a complete and utter brat! For someone who claims she gets no attention from her parents, she sure acts like a spoiled baby. *You shall do this, you shall not do that. You shall not do anything that annoys me in the slightest way. Because I, Eve, am special and talented and the whole world shall revolve around me.*

Yeah, Eve, I rage, *get a clue. Maybe you're not so special. Maybe you're not so talented. Maybe you're just an egomaniac who gets off on bossing everyone around.*

And Anna. I love Anna, but what a wimp! Standing there while Eve went off, going, "Oh, uh, oh, uh." Gee, thanks, Anna! Really helpful! Whoever's the most powerful person in the room, that's who she listens to. Not the person who's right, not the person who needs help—the one who's yelling loudest. When she was stage manager for *Cabaret*, she just ran around doing everyone's bidding. Never once said, *No, do it yourself!* No wonder she gets into man messes all the time. She can't stand up for herself. Has to have someone to please.

You know what? If they never call me again? Good. Fine. Not the end of the world.

And Mark . . . somehow I'm mad at him, too. I want to be happy that he kissed me, replay the scene in my head a thousand times. Only I can't because I bet after all that screaming, he never speaks to me again. Mark hates screaming. I know because I hate it too.

By the time I get home, the anger's burned up all my energy. I'm exhausted, empty. A strong wind could blow me anywhere. When I open the door and Beesley doesn't come creeping down the hall to greet me, I fight hard not to start crying again.

With no more rage surging through me, I feel remorse. Of course Eve doesn't want me dating her brother. How could I have been so insensitive when she just went through this hideous audition? And how could I have been so nasty to Anna, throwing Declan and Nelson in her face? What kind of warped person am I?

I never unpacked from the trip. Now I empty my bag all over my bed. My scrapbook falls open to a picture of my dad with Widget. I throw it across the room, then feel terrible. I rescue it from the corner. That seems to be all I do these days—blow up, then feel guilty.

In the mess I find the postcard Mr. Courtney wrote, promising to send info on Julliard. I tear it into pieces, toss them in the trash.

I need the phone to ring more than anything. Some sign that I have not been permanently exiled from the human race. I want to call Anna to find out what happened after I left, but it's not fair to put her in the middle. *Really* can't call Eve. Maybe . . .

Before I have time to think, I start dialing Eve's number. If Eve answers, I'll simply hang up. Or say that I'm sorry. Or—

A click. "Hello?"

Oh, boy. Mrs. Baylor. Stammering, I say, "Hi, M-Mrs. Baylor, it's—"

"Syd, hello!" Mrs. Baylor sounds all happy to hear from me. Clearly, she doesn't know her daughter now hates my guts. "You want Eve, hold on. . . ."

I say desperately, "No, Mrs. Baylor, actually . . . I, uh, wanted to talk to Mark. If he's there."

"Mark?" Now Mrs. B's confused. But she says,

"Hold on." Then, to my utter horror, she shouts, "Mark, honey! Sydney Callender for you."

A long pause during which I wonder if it is possible to die from embarrassment. The silence is broken by Eve yelling down the hall, "Oh, Marky Mark, your beloved is calling" and Mark yelling, "Shut up!"

Taking the phone, he says pointedly, "Thanks, Mom."

Another pause. Then, "Hi."

If there was a worse way for this conversation to start, I can't imagine it. Carefully, I say "Hi" back. Then, "Is this not a good time?"

"No, just . . ." He sighs. "My family's insane, what else is new? How are you?" His voice is impatient, and I feel like any answer I give will bore him.

So I keep it short. "I'm okay."

"Yeah? You . . . got home and everything?"

He's struggling to come up with things to say. Which makes me uncomfortable. All I can manage is "Yeah . . . I only live a few blocks away."

"Oh, right."

Now he's insulted. I adore Mark, but I already know he hates feeling stupid. Smart is the one thing he has— at least that's how he sees it. Nervous, I babble, "Of course, there's no way you'd know that. I mean, why would you? It's not in the least bit important."

A long, horrible silence. Then, "Right." Like he doesn't know what to say.

This is such a disaster, the only thing to do is end it before it gets any worse. "Well, look, I just wanted to thank you for being nice to me today and say . . . I'm okay now, I'm fine, and . . ."

I hesitate, feeling somehow I'm saying something I don't want to say. I throw out, "So."

"So," echoes Mark.

Through the silence, I beg him, *Please say something. Please don't think I'm a dork. If I've done something wrong, please know that I'm useless at stuff like this. It scares me, and I don't know how to do it. But it's not that I don't like you, because I do. . . .*

There's a knock at the door. Confused, I call out, "What?"

Hear my dad say, "It's me."

Instantly, Mark says, "I should let you go."

I want to yell, *No!* But I'm distracted by my dad at the door; I don't want him hearing me talk to Mark. So I say, "Um, okay, but . . . maybe we'll talk later?"

"Yeah," says Mark offhandedly. "Bye."

Miserable, I hang up. Guys don't like drama. And between dead cats, bursting into tears, Eve throwing tantrums, and his mom being all curious, I've been nothing but drama.

And now my dad wants attention, when he's the last person I want to think about.

Opening the door, my dad looks in. "Am I interrupting?"

"No," I say shortly.

He leans against the wall. "I wanted to ask how the funeral went."

Like he cares. "Fine."

My dad nods, waits for more. When it doesn't come, he puts his hands on the doorknob, turns it. "I thought maybe we could make a donation. In Beesley's memory. To the Humane Society or whatever you think would be—"

The rage is back. *Write a check and everything will be fine, huh?* I say, "Why?"

"Well, to—"

"It doesn't change anything," I snap. "It doesn't make anything better."

My dad nods once. "I know."

"So why do it?" My dad opens his mouth to answer. "Don't. Really. Don't. I don't want to talk about this with you."

He drops his head, takes a deep breath. "Syd, I don't know how to say I'm sorry for this."

"If you don't know, then don't try." My dad

flinches. I have never spoken to my dad that way. It feels good. Strong.

"I screwed up. Bad. I know that."

Screwed up. It's like a little kid. *I screwed up.* That's what you say when something breaks, not when something dies. "Okay."

My dad rubs his hand over his face. "Okay? That's all I get: okay?"

For "screwed up"? I think. *Yeah, that's all you get.*

I stand up. "Here's how it is. You don't know how to say you're sorry, I don't know how to say it doesn't matter. So, really, I don't even know what we're talking about."

I open the door, say, "Could you leave now? Go away. Please."

The next morning the phone rings, and I pounce on it. When I hear Anna's voice my relief is so intense, I think I'll faint.

She says, "God, that was . . ."

"Weird."

"Yeah. You want to meet for breakfast?"

"Absolutely."

As I leave to meet Anna, I see my dad sitting at the kitchen table. He's still in his pajamas. Usually, he's dressed by now. I guess he figures since he has no job to go to anymore, why bother?

Not my problem, I think as I slam out the door.

At Fluff's, I order a bagel and a smoothie. Anna has a doughnut. When we settle in at a table, I take the plunge and ask, "Have you talked to Eve at all?"

Anna hesitates. "Uh, she called."

"And?"

Anna tosses her head this way and that as if she's trying to figure out how much truth I can take. "You know, she's psycho about the whole boyfriend thing, and then she's psycho about the whole Mark thing, so this is like . . . double psychosis."

"Right." Then, to test, "I guess I majorly screwed up."

I throw in the "majorly," hoping Anna will say, *No, come on . . .* But instead, I get silence.

Miserable, I say, "I'm sorry."

"No, it's just . . ." Anna sighs. "It's so not your fault, but, of course, Eve is angry at me because she's convinced I knew all along—which I kind of did—so she was like, 'How could you not tell me?' And I couldn't say because it was a secret, because that would make her even more insane."

"I'm really sorry."

"Then, of course, she had to say that I could never

speak to you again." My stomach drops. "And, of course, I said, 'That's not happening.' But if you want to know how she's feeling, that's how she's feeling. She's upset—not pretend upset, the way we know she can be . . ."

Eve hates me, I think. *One of my two best friends in the whole world hates me. And my other best friend is stuck in the middle.* I say it again. "I'm sorry."

Anna says, "The only thing I can say is she did the same thing to me with Declan. And for better or worse, we're still friends."

"Declan wasn't her brother," I point out.

"No—true." There's nowhere we can go from here, so Anna changes the subject. "So, what's up with you and Mark? Did you guys talk?"

I slump in my seat. "Yeah. It didn't go too well."

"Why not?"

I give her a blow-by-blow account of our conversation. As she listens, Anna nods, raises eyebrows, and quirks her mouth disapprovingly. "What do you think?" I say finally.

Anna chews her lower lip. "Um . . ."

"Be honest."

"Okay. I think Mark likes you. But as someone who has dated a reformed geek"—Declan—"and a hard-core geek"—Nelson—"I have to tell you: They don't know how to act."

Anna's so serious, I smile a little. "What do you mean?"

"Like . . . guys are weird anyway, right? The basic things girls know how to do, they don't know. Well, geeks really don't know. It's not that they don't care. But they're scared. So they want you to do all the nice stuff: the inviting, the compliments. And that can be nice, but it can also be a drag, because you never really know how they feel. And because they don't know how to act, they can hurt you. Like Nelson just saying, 'Oh, by the way, I'm leaving' without thinking, 'Hey, maybe that's a big deal.'"

I remember how I felt on the phone, wanting so bad for Mark to come out of his shell and say, *I like you. Let's do this.* But he never did. Maybe Anna's onto something.

I say, "So, what—we don't get scared?"

"Not the same way."

"I do, I think."

"Yeah, but you've never hurt someone because you're scared. You never not come through for people."

Tearing up a napkin, I think, *I didn't come through for Beesley.* But that wasn't because I was scared, just stupid.

Anna says, "All I'm saying is, if you want it to

happen with Mark, be prepared for a lot of 'God, what is he thinking?' conversations like that one."

I chew a piece of bagel. As crazy as I am about Mark, I don't know if I can deal with that. Particularly now. I need to know what's happening. Secrets make me crazy. I think of the fantasy girlfriend I came up with for Mark a few months ago. The gorgeous computer-savvy chick. She'd just cut through all of Mark's "Right's" and "So's."

So why can't I? I finger my cell phone in my bag. Because . . . I can't.

Then I hear Anna say, "I feel like a total rat." I look up at her. "But I have to go. It's summer switch-over time, and my dad's picking us up at eleven."

Summer switch-over. The time when Anna and Russell go stay with her dad, and it's understood we won't see her as much because he lives on the other side of town. I clamp my teeth on my tongue to keep from saying, *You know, maybe you could not go to your dad's this year. Because you're the one sane person in my life right now, and I really need you.*

But as I watch Anna gather her stuff, I know I have to let her go. And maybe it's my imagination, but she seems relieved that she won't have to deal with me and Eve for the next few weeks. Can't say I blame her.

We hurry back to our building to find Mr. Morris

waiting for her on the street. Seeing us, Russell jumps up and down, shrieking, "There she is, there she is, there she is!"

"Hi, Daddy." Anna goes up to her dad, gets a big hug.

That feels like my cue to exit, so I wave good-bye. "Have a great time."

Anna grabs me by the hand. "Daddy, can Syd come to dinner sometime?"

"Of course," says her father.

But Russell wails, "No! Just us. I want it just us, Daddy."

Anna wheels on him. "Shut up, Russell!" Russell bursts into tears.

Her father says, "A little harsh, Anna."

Feeling like a total jinx—another happy family wrecked by the amazing Sydney!—I say quickly, "I'll call you, okay?"

Torn between me and her dad, Anna nods uncertainly, then goes to apologize to Russell. I back away, still waving, but she's pretending to be an orangutan for Russell and doesn't see me.

It's funny—when the cards predicted absence or separation, Anna was the one who got most upset. Now she's gone away, for the most normal reason on earth, but she is absent. I tell myself she'll be back in three weeks, it's not like she's gone forever. But with Eve not talking to me, who knows what will happen? It was always the three of us: me, Anna, and Eve. If Eve doesn't forgive me, Anna will still say she's my friend, but she and Eve go to the same school. She needs Eve. After a while it'll just be easier not to see me. Like my mom said, things change.

When I get home, I walk past my dad's study. The door's closed, but the light's on.

Fine.

And that's where he stays. For the next week it's like we have an unseen guest in the house. We're not sure how he got here or when he's leaving, and it seems best to just pretend he's not around. He doesn't even show up for dinner anymore. The first few nights, my mom went and knocked on the door. Then she stopped bothering. We're eating a lot of takeout.

Usually, when my dad gets down, he plays a lot. But the piano is silent.

Sometimes I think, *Well, this can't go on.* Then I wonder, *Why not? What's going to stop it?*

One night I open my door to go to the bathroom, and I hear my mom talking. She's in the study, trying to keep her voice low, but I can make out some of what she's saying.

". . . won't put up with this forever."

Then my dad: "Put up with what?"

Nothing for a moment. Then my mom asking, "Have you tried talking to her?"

Her. I am her. They're talking about me. Whatever my dad says, I don't hear. Only my mom saying, "Maybe try again."

Then my dad saying back, "What's the use?"

"So, what's the plan, Ted? Just sit here?"

"What does it matter?"

For a long time, silence. When I next hear my mom, her voice is louder. "Something has to matter, Ted. If not your job, then how about those kids you signed on to teach? If not those kids, how about your own kid? And, while I'm on the subject, how about me?"

If my dad answers, I don't hear it. All I hear is my mom slamming the door behind her. Quietly, I shut my door, get into bed, curl up in a ball.

The next thing I know, I'm woken up by a sharp knock at the door. Not my mom. Too high and hard for my mom. Pulling the covers close, I say, "Come in."

My dad opens the door. But he doesn't come in. He doesn't turn on the light. He just stands there. For a weird second I feel scared. Like he's a stranger and could do anything.

He's holding on to the doorknob with one hand,

the wall with the other, like he'd fall over if he didn't. I wonder if my mom's still awake, if I should go get her.

Then he takes his hand off the wall and points at me.

"God," he says. "You and your *mother*."

Then he slams the door shut.

I stare at the ceiling for what seems like hours. I never felt safe in the world. But I felt safe at home. Because of my dad. He made a place for me in the world and I knew I was okay here.

Now I get it, what the cards meant. I've been living in a fantasy. Because nowhere is safe, not even your own little corner.

I miss Beesley in the worst way.

I miss everybody.

The next morning I have to go somewhere, anywhere. I cannot be in the house when my dad gets up, I can't. So I get on the bus and go to Liz's clinic.

I don't know what I think Liz can do. But I feel like she's the only person who's outside the insanity right now. There's no one else I can ask: *Is this just how it is? The way things will be for the rest of my life? Because this is crazy—isn't it?*

Liz's clinic is always full—partly because she can't say no to anyone and mostly because she's a terrific doctor. Already waiting are three cats in carriers, one Chihuahua, one Rottweiler with a bandage on its paw, and an adorable long-haired mutt squirming and whimpering in its owner's lap. Some animals sense when they're in a place for the sick, and it freaks them out. Just like most people hate hospitals.

Liz's assistant, Rosie, is rushing around with a clipboard, taking down information about each patient. I don't see Liz anywhere; she must be in the back. I wait by the door for Rosie to notice me, but she's too busy soothing a cat owner who feels she's waited too long. I sit down, thinking maybe Rosie will mistake me for a client and come over.

Which she does, saying, "Okay, sweetie, now . . ."

"Hey, Rosie, it's me."

She looks up from the clipboard, slaps a hand to her forehead. "Sydney, I'm so sorry! It's madness today. What can I do for you? I was so sorry to hear about Beesley."

"Thanks. No, I was wondering . . ."

Just then the Rottweiler pees all over the floor in a giant gush, and everyone yells and pushes their chairs back. "Hold on a second, honey," says Rosie. Rushing to the back, she calls out, "That's why God invented paper towels!"

It is funny, and even I laugh a little. But as I watch

Rosie mop up the spill, then calm a maddened cockatoo, I realize everyone here is way too busy to talk to me. What did I expect? That Liz was going to come out and say, *Okay, everyone, go home! Sydney here has a big problem, and I need to listen to her for hours and hours . . . ?*

I slip out the door without Rosie noticing.

To stretch out my trip home, I decide to walk through the park. What's weird about Central Park is that there are so many people and yet you can feel totally alone. As I walk around the reservoir, I see joggers, moms with their strollers, little kids, vendors selling ice cream, people on their coffee or lunch breaks, laughing on benches and eating yogurt out of paper bags.

I pass by a dog run, and a German shepherd bounds up to me. I put my hand out, say, "Hey, guy." But he must smell how screwed up I am because he puts his head to one side like, *What's up with you, lady?* and runs to join the other dogs.

Without thinking, I get out my cell phone, punch in the number for Anna's dad's house. It rings and rings until the machine picks up and Mr. Morris's voice says, "Hi, I'm not here right now . . ." I hang up before the beep.

Then, as fast as possible, so I don't even have to really admit what I'm doing, I dial Eve's number. But when I hear Eve's voice say, "Hello?" I shut my cell phone immediately.

It would be nice if the park were just endless. If you could walk and walk and never get home....

The second I walk through the door, I can feel something's wrong. I don't know what it is. Something is off. For a moment I think, *Burglars.* If you think the house has been robbed, you're supposed to walk right out and call the police. Do not go inside, because they might still be there.

But the door isn't bashed in or anything, which you'd think would be the case if someone broke in. Closing it, I call, "Hello?"

No answer.

My dad's like me. He doesn't have anywhere to go either. So I call, "Dad?"

Silence. I call again, "Dad?

Maybe he's out, I think. *Maybe any second now, he'll come back and I'll realize this is just another example of how I turn everything into a horror film.*

But I can't explain it. The emptiness of the house feels wrong. The silence feels wrong. It's the silence after something awful happens and no one knows what to do or say.

Check every room. That's all I can do. The something wrong has to be in one of these rooms. If I don't find it, then everything's fine. First the kitchen . . .

Go away, Sydney.

Not there. Down the hallway to the living room.

I'm sorry, honey.

My parents' room. My dad's study.

Marty called me from school. I know what happened.

By the time I get to the bathroom, I know I've made the whole thing up. There is no drama here, no catastrophe. Once again, Syd the scaredy-cat has flipped for no reason.

But then I see my dad lying on the tiled floor, see the blood, and I know the disaster I've been waiting for all my life has finally come.

ELEVEN
ACE OF SWORDS, SIDEWAYS
Love, success or disaster, self-destruction

I have never been in a hospital before.

And now here I am. In a hospital.

It's different from what I thought it would be like. For one thing, it's noisier. You know how in movies and on TV, there're all these caring doctors holding your hand, explaining everything in detail, and saying, "I'm so sorry, Mrs. Peterson"? Doesn't happen. These doctors act like talking to you is a big waste of time. Like they're offended when you say, "Is my dad dead or what?"

It's one of those things I always thought about, how I would deal if something happened to my parents. What would I do if one of them were sick or died?

Now my dad is in the hospital.

And I don't know how I'm dealing.

I'm not crying. I'm not screaming. But it's not because I'm being so strong or together; it's that I don't feel anything. Just shut off somehow.

In the waiting room there's this woman who's yelling into her cell phone. I wish she would shut up. *We don't all need to hear you,* I want to tell her.

Liz is here. She's sitting next to me like that's her job while my mother tries to find someone who will tell her something. She's noticing me notice the woman on the phone, and she says, "Lady's got a loud mouth." I nod.

Good thing my dad has a kid who has no friends. Otherwise, he could have bled to death, right there on the bathroom floor. Then where would he be? Where would we be?

"I'm getting a soda," says Liz. "You want something?"

"No, thanks."

Now the woman has hung up the phone and gone over to yell at the nurse. The nurse looks annoyed. I hope she throws the woman out.

Liz gets up. "I'm going anyway. You sure?"

I nod. "Yeah, sure."

At first I was absolutely sure he was dead. He was

on the floor, there was blood all over, blood on the sink. And puke as well, if you want to know. I guess I can't say anymore that my dad isn't a drunk because he doesn't puke. Although Liz says he probably threw up after, from the shock of hitting his head.

"And then he passed out?" I asked her.

She said, "Probably."

There are things I don't ever want to do again. One of them is touch someone's neck to see if they have a pulse. If they ask me to do it again in biology or swim class, I'm going to say no. And if they push it, I'm going to tell them why I said no.

Liz's back. She's gotten me a Kit Kat, even though I told her I didn't want anything. I don't want to hurt her feelings, so I eat half.

She tells me my mom talked to the doctors, and apparently, my dad is not dead.

"She's gone up to see him."

I nod.

"But they can't let you go up 'cause you are under-age." She says this last part like she's a Southern sheriff: *Uhnda-aige.*

Then she says, "Sorry, kiddo."

"I'm not sorry."

I can feel it: Liz has a hug she wants to give me. I really, really don't want it. I'm worried I might shriek if she tries. But I made a mistake, saying what I did, that "I'm not sorry," because it was too mean, too angry, and people think a hug takes care of mean and angry. Even smart people like Liz. Or I guess they don't know what else to do. I mean, how many Kit Kats can Liz get me?

So I get the hug and I take it. It's not too bad. I knew it was coming, so all that happens is my throat aches like I tried to swallow a fork.

Liz says, "This was a bad day."

And I say, "That it was."

A little while later my mom comes down. As she gets off the elevator, it seems she doesn't know where to go. Then she rushes to me and holds me for a very long time. Then she says into my hair, "Okay . . . okay . . ."

I want to ask, *What is okay?*

Stepping back, she says, "Uh, look. I'm going to stay here tonight. I want to be here when your dad wakes up. So you'll be sleeping over at Liz's—okay?"

I nod, thinking, *Oh, lucky Liz. The Callender family has a disaster, and it turns into her problem.* I wonder if that's what we'll become. The disaster family everyone feels sorry for. I wonder if that's what we've been.

When the time comes for us to leave the hospital while my mom stays, we just sort of stand there. Then Mom leans in and gives me a hug. "Love you," she says.

I'm supposed to say it back. But there's something wrong with it, and I can't. Like, *Oh, we're in the hospital, and Dad almost died, but isn't it great—we all love each other!*

On the drive home Liz asks, "Japanese for dinner?" and I say, "Fine." Then we both watch the traffic.

Liz's cell phone rings and she picks up. This makes me nervous—you're not supposed to drive and talk at the same time. So I listen closely as Liz says, "Oh, hi. Everything all right?" She pauses. "Phew." She smiles at me, and I guess that it's my mom on the phone.

Then she says, "Oh. I see. No, I agree, that'd be better. Yeah. Sounds good. Will do. Big hug."

Clicking off, she says, "Change of plans."

I try to smile, hide my disappointment. Even though I knew I couldn't hide out at Liz's forever, I had this vision of eating vegetable tempura and going to sleep on Liz's couch, surrounded by her dogs, Brownie and Layla . . . you know, for the rest of my life.

But clearly, my mom has decided she should be home with her little girl.

Liz turns the car around, and we head back through the park. As we wait in traffic, Liz says, "I need you to do me a favor."

"What?"

"Go easy on your mom, okay?" She holds up a hand. "I'm not saying she's done everything the way I would have done it or you would have done it. I'm just saying that right now this mess is on her shoulders, and it's not a mess she made." She gives me a long look. "You know what I'm saying?"

I do. She's saying my dad made this mess. But I'm not so much angry at my dad as I feel he doesn't exist anymore. But that's too much to explain to Liz right now.

"I'll try," I tell her. Only, when I think about trying—facing my mom tonight and listening to her talk about my dad, who I never want to talk about again—I feel exhausted.

As we drive up my block, I notice someone familiar standing outside the building. Sitting up so I can see better, I realize it's Anna. What is she doing here? For a second I have this horrible fear that something happened to her and she had to come home early.

Then she sees me, starts waving. And I realize, *She's here for me. Anna is my change of plans.*

Then I see Eve come out of the lobby. All of a sudden, I'm ashamed. It's too big, what she's doing. Maybe no one else would see it that way. But Eve never gives up on a fight—ever. So her being here feels like the most overwhelming thing anyone could do for me.

Eve bangs on the car window. "Hey, you—get out here."

Totally confused, I get out of the car. "Uh, hi."

"Hi," Anna and Eve say together.

Then Eve says, "You suck, you know that?"

"Not telling us," adds Anna.

"Like, we're only your best friends," says Eve. "Right?" she says menacingly.

I swallow. "I'm sorry, guys, it was all . . ."

"Forget it." Anna loops her arm through mine. "Your mom called and told my mom what happened. So we decided: sleepover at my house."

Sleepover at Anna's. There is no way I will ever be able to tell Anna how much that means to me, how saved I feel.

I hug Liz. Over my shoulder, she says to Anna and Eve, "You guys are good people."

Anna says, "Syd's great people."

"That she is," says Liz, giving me a squeeze.

As we take the elevator up to Anna's apartment, Anna says, "We thought maybe we'd order from that new Chinese place, Tofu Palace."

"Great." For Anna and Eve to try anything even remotely tofu related is a big sacrifice.

"Also, we got a movie," says Eve.

"We weren't sure what you'd feel like . . . ," says Anna.

"So we got *Babe*," finishes Eve.

I smile. *Babe* is my all-time favorite movie; I've seen it a hundred times. Eve hates it—or pretends she does. The one time we watched it together, she kept yelling "Bacon!" at the screen.

Again, I say, "Great!"

In her room Anna drags all her big pillows onto the floor, and we lie back and watch. No one says a word—not even Eve.

Halfway through the movie, I say, "Eve?"

"Yeah?"

"You can yell 'bacon' if you want to."

For the first time that night, everyone laughs.

Sleepovers at Anna's mean Anna gets her bed, Eve gets her sleeping bag, and I take her foldout futon chair. As I huddle under the blankets, Mouli comes padding over to me. He's got a scowl on his striped orange face. For a moment he glares at me, and I wonder if he's mad that Beesley is gone, if somehow he thinks it's my fault.

I'm sorry, Mouli, I think. *I'm sorry I let your friend down.*

Mouli looks away as if he's trying to decide what he thinks of this. Then, all of a sudden, he lies down next to the futon. I reach out, stroke the stripes on his back.

Standing by the light switch, Anna says, "Ready?"

Eve straightens herself in the sleeping bag, shuts her eyes. "Ready."

"Ready," I say. It's our ritual. Everyone has to agree to lights-out. The room goes dark, and I see Anna tiptoe her way to bed. For a while everyone's quiet. I think of my dad, what he's doing now. Maybe the doctors were wrong and he was worse than they thought and he's dead and my mom's at the hospital freaking out. In the morning there'll be a call. Anna's mom saying shakily, *Syd, I have some terrible news.*

Or, I guess, she'd put me on the phone, let my mom tell me. If she does tell me that, I think I'll just hang up on her.

Then I hear Eve say, "I want to do Truth."

Truth is our sleepover game. In the dark everyone has to say one thing that's absolutely true about themselves, and the other two have to accept it. It can be something you think, something you want, something you hate. Like, once my truth was that I was mad at Eve for making fun of me. It's a way of making sure we don't have secrets from one another.

"Shoot," says Anna.

Eve says, "Truth: Syd, I think you're scary brave.

Like, I always believed you when you said you were chicken about things? I thought, 'Yes, I am the brave one, the tough one.' But . . . wrong. You make me feel like a stupid little kid, the stuff you're dealing with."

I smile. "Truth: You're not a stupid little kid. You're still the tough one."

"Well, you're the tough one too."

"I'll be the chicken," volunteers Anna, and we laugh.

Then Anna blurts out, "Truth: I'm scared. I want your dad to be okay."

I think of my reading, the Death card. It could have meant Beesley, because that was the last time I felt anything for my dad. Death of Beesley, death of my feelings. Or it could mean . . .

I roll over, stare up at the ceiling. "Truth: I'm not brave. I'm not brave because I'm not scared. I don't care anymore."

After that, no one says anything. In the darkness I think, *My whole life, I've been scared of being out there. In the world. I was scared to do a reading because I didn't want to know. All that fear . . . didn't stop it from happening.*

And now I'm in the world. Now I know the things I was scared to find out.

But I'm still here. Eve and Anna are still here.

At some point I fall asleep.

TWELVE

KNIGHT OF WANDS

Journey, advance into the unknown, absence

In the morning Anna makes me promise: "Call me every day, Miss Sydney." I laugh. "I mean it. If I don't hear from you, I'll bang down your door."

"Okay," I say.

Eve has been hanging back a little. I guess she still feels strange about what happened with Mark; no big surprise, so do I. Now she steps up, gives me a fierce hug, and says, "If you're ever in trouble and don't call me, I will seriously hurt you."

Trying to keep a straight face, I say, "Thank you? I guess?"

Anna joins the hug, and for a moment we three stand together, heads touching, staring down at our feet. Then Eve says, "Anna, those are some ugly shoes," and we crack up laughing.

Then I take the elevator home. It's only a few floors, but it feels like a different universe.

My mom meets me at the door, hugging me like she hasn't seen me in years. Then she takes a big breath and says, "Dad's okay."

I say, "Good."

"He's out of the ICU."

I give my mom another "Good."

My mom frowns. There's something she wants that I'm not giving her. The "Goods" are not enough. But that's all I have right now.

Then she says, "You want some breakfast?"

I ate at Anna's, but since Liz asked me to be nice to my mom, I say, "Okay."

As I drink a glass of orange juice, Mom says she's taking time off from work, so she can be home and deal with my dad. "It's going to be different, I promise."

I say, "Fine," because I can't stay with the "Goods." She doesn't like the "Goods."

"Your dad's going to get help. For his drinking. And the anger. He's going to go to a clinic."

"Fine." It's like a weird game of catch. My mom keeps throwing me the ball, I keep letting it drop.

"He promised to stop," my mom tells me. "He knows he has a problem."

"Fine."

The ball's dead on the floor. We can both feel it. I don't know what my mom expects. Big smiles? Crying? *Oh, thank God, thank God? Of course he's going to a clinic,* I want to say. *He knows he has to do something to make us like him again, he isn't stupid.*

My mom gets all busy setting out cereal and putting the bowls on the table. When there's nothing left to do, she sits down. Pouring herself some coffee, she says, "He says hi."

I turn my spoon over. "That's nice."

"He understands if you don't want to see him. He wanted me to tell you that if he were you, he wouldn't want to see him either."

This makes me sad. This is my dad's "I'm an adult who's smart enough to know how dumb adults can be" routine. It used to work. Before *I* knew how dumb adults can be.

Questions are dangerous. They show you care. But I ask anyway. "Do you think this will work?"

My mom pauses before answering. "I think your dad is going to try harder at this than he has at anything in his life."

I say, "Try."

"That's all he can promise, honey." She puts her hand on mine. I wish she wouldn't. It's like she's holding me down, making me listen as she explains that Dad will be at this clinic for two weeks. Apparently, that's how long it takes. Whatever it is they'll do to him. We're not allowed to see him for the first week. Fine with me.

When she's finished explaining, my mom waits. I guess this is the part where I'm supposed to say something. But nothing's coming. I have a flash of my dad. *I'm not going to pretend* . . . Well, I can't pretend either— even for him.

Taking her hand away, Mom says, "Say something, Sydney. Please."

"Like what?"

Mom takes a deep breath. "I know it was very hard for you, losing Beesley." I shake my head. I don't want to talk about Beesley with someone who didn't like him. "But that wasn't your father's fault."

I wait for a moment, then say, "You know what, Mom? You're right. It wasn't Dad's fault. It was mine."

"No . . ."

"*You* told me: Don't leave him with Dad. You knew it was a bad idea. So you're absolutely right. My fault completely."

"Sydney, I said that because I knew Beesley was old and sick, and if anything happened, you'd never forgive yourself—or, frankly, anyone else. Your dad's . . ." She struggles. "Sometimes, when you're older, you hit a point in your life when you realize that your dreams might not happen. And it's hard."

"So he makes life hard for everybody else," I say flatly.

My mom sighs. "Sometimes, my darling, you can have a very puritan attitude. You know what I mean by that? Judgmental, black and white. It's easy with animals. They're simple, they're helpless. People are a lot more complicated. The best people, the *best* of them, Syd, will screw up. Including you. It's a hard thing to face, and sometimes I think people who like animals more than people don't want to deal with that complexity. They think, 'Animals good, people bad.' But people aren't bad, Sydney, they're just complicated. And they need our help just as much as those cats and dogs you love so much."

"This is a joke," I tell her. "You get mad at Dad all the time."

Trying to keep her voice low, my mom says, "Yes. I know I do. But I am trying to get past anger right now, Sydney, so we can get your dad some help."

"Well, that's great for you," I say. "But you didn't—"

All of a sudden, I can't speak. Memories of Beesley too sick to look up come flooding into my head. I try again, "You didn't—"

But I can't say it. Wiping tears away, I try to get up. But my mom blocks me. At first I hate that she's in my way. I want to push her, hard. But then she becomes something to hold on to, which is good, because suddenly, all I want to do is cry. Cry for everything and everyone that's gone, cry for the fact that creatures die, that feelings die, that things don't stay the same.

My mom is cooing "Okay . . . okay . . ." and rubbing my hair. Stepping back a bit, she says, "Better?"

Which is sort of funny, like, *Oh, yeah, all better now!* So I laugh a bit. And weirdly, I do feel better.

But it's not like anything's changed, so I say, "Um, not really."

My mom smiles. "I know. Me neither." I laugh again. "But we will be. I promise, honey. It won't be the same, but . . . in a way, is that the worst thing? I know there are some things about the past I could stand to lose."

I think of my dad standing at my door, pointing his finger. *God, you and your mother.* I nod. "Yeah, definitely."

"We'll make a list," says Mom. "Things we'll keep, things we'll get rid of."

I smile. "Music—keep."

"Anger—"

"Get rid of." I hesitate. "Disappointment?"

"Live with." She strokes my hair. "Get past. Move on."

It's funny. Those are words I always hated hearing from my mom. "Get past it, you have to move on." Like you should never be attached to anything or care too much. But when she says it now, the death grip around my heart loosens. Maybe sometimes, when there's nothing you can do, maybe you have to learn to care a little less?

I'm wondering how I feel about this when my mom says, "Hey, I forgot, there's a letter for you."

"Me?" I never get letters.

She goes to the table by the door where we always throw the mail. Taking out an envelope, she reads, "William Courtney?" She raises an eyebrow. "Secret admirer?"

At first the William throws me. Then I remember: Mr. Courtney. The music teacher at Anna and Eve's school who made a big deal about my playing.

Taking the envelope, I say, "He did the musical where I played the piano."

"The one who thought you should do the summer program at Julliard." My mom hasn't forgotten.

"Yeah, that one." I open the envelope. Inside is a brochure with a big yellow Post-it: *Here's what you're missing, young lady! Get out from under that bushel! There's always next summer. With sincere admiration, William Courtney.*

I can hear his Southern accent even in the note. "He's so nuts," I say.

"Doesn't sound nuts to me," says my mom lightly, reading over my shoulder.

Setting the brochure aside, I say, "Mom, really. I know you mean to be nice, but Julliard's not for me."

"Who says?" asks my mom. "Your dad? Let me tell you something, Sydney. Just because your father couldn't handle Julliard doesn't mean you can't."

Okay, this is flippy. Suddenly, my mom believes in me? Puzzled, I say, "Mom, Dad's a genius, I'm totally average."

"Oh, really? I don't think Mr. Courtney would be sending that to a girl who's totally average." Before I can tell her she's nuts too, she says, "Do me a favor, Sydney. Yes, another favor, I know I'm asking a lot of them recently. But this one I really want, okay?"

She waits until I say, "Okay."

"Don't believe your dad when he says the world's a big, scary place full of mean, ugly people. Don't believe him when he says you can't handle it." She takes me by the arms. "You can handle anything. You handled yesterday, didn't you?"

"Didn't have a choice," I remind her.

"But you're still standing, aren't you? And if you can stay standing after that, what's Julliard got that's so scary? Look, Syd, maybe I don't know music the way your father does; I know I don't. But I do know my daughter. And I *know* she's anything but average."

My mom is so intense, I feel a little embarrassed. "Okay, but she's still a scaredy-cat."

"Is she?" My mom takes my hands, looks into my eyes. "Are those really your fears, Sydney? Or are you borrowing them from someone else? In which case, maybe it's time to give them back?"

My mom has to go into her office to make sure everyone knows what they're supposed to do while she's away. I wash the dishes from lunch and tidy up the kitchen. Picking up the Julliard brochure, I wonder how I can throw it away without my mom noticing. What she said was incredibly sweet . . . but she's still nuts.

I hold it, ready to rip it up. Then I see Mr. Courtney's note. I can't tear that up. It's too nice. I can't believe he bothered to remember me.

But he did, I realize. So, maybe even if I don't believe something, it can still be true?

And maybe if I believe something bad, I'm not always right?

Are those your fears, Sydney? Or someone else's?

I tuck the brochure in with our take-out menus. I'll throw it away some other time.

I know I should feel sad that my dad's in the hospital, but I'm not (which, weirdly, does make me a little sad). I realize that for the past few weeks I've been like Beesley—nervous, creeping around, not sure what's around the corner. Now it's like we've thrown open all the windows and said, *Let's get some light and air in here.*

And the strangest thing of all? I actually like hanging out with my mom. One Saturday morning I even watch some *Desperate Housewives* episodes that she TiVo'd. During a commercial, she asks, "What do you think?"

Not wanting to hurt her feelings, I say, "They seem a little goofy to me. I like the one who works, though." She just laughs.

During the next commercial, she says, "You know, I was thinking maybe Monday we could drop by Lincoln Center, check out . . . Julliard." She wiggles her eyebrows.

I smile. "Mom."

"Dare you."

"Hello, I'm not six years old."

"Double dare you."

"Mom . . ."

The phone rings. My mom tenses up. She's thinking the same thing I am: What if it's the clinic? What if something's happened to my dad? The phone's nearest me, so I pick up, say, "Hello?"

And hear Eve say, "Syd?"

Not the hospital. I signal to my mom and say, "Eve, what's up?"

"It's Tat, she's sick."

"What's wrong with her?"

"I don't know, I don't know," Eve says fretfully. "She's just panting and miserable and . . . I don't know, I'm scared she's going to die. Can you come over?"

But I have a better idea. I give Eve the address of Liz's clinic and tell her to meet me there in half an hour.

As I hang up, my mom says, "Those girls really rely on you, don't they?"

"I think I rely on them more," I say.

"Well, that's how it should be with good friends." She smiles. "I'm glad you have them. I hope you always do."

By the time I get to the clinic, Eve is already waiting outside with Tat's carrier. Anna is right behind her. Poor Anna, she's getting no time with her dad this summer.

"Look at her," says Eve. "You'll see right away, she's not well."

"Or," says Anna patiently, "she hates the summer heat."

"That's not it," says Eve shrilly. "I know it. There's something really wrong."

I peek inside the carrier. Normally, Tat in her carrier is a bristling ball of green-eyed attitude. But she's just lying there, eyes half closed and panting. "She doesn't seem like herself."

"See?" Eve turns to Anna.

"But it could be the heat. All that fur. Is she getting enough water?"

Eve nods. "I even tried giving her Gatorade."

Maybe not the best thing, but no point in telling Eve that now. Leading everyone into the clinic, I say, "I'm sure Liz will figure this out, don't worry."

"Like . . . now," says Eve anxiously.

I nod, even though I'm sure there are others in front of us on line and there's no way Tat's going to get right in. But poor Eve is so frantic, I feel like anything I can do or say to reassure her is worth it. As I head to the front desk to put Tat's name on the waiting list, it occurs to me that Tat is the first thing Eve has really ever cared about that she couldn't walk away from. When she gets in fights with me or Anna, she always claims she'll be fine if she never sees us again. We know it's not true, but Eve likes to believe it.

But I guess this is different. As I watch her talking softly to the carrier, telling Tat she's going to be seen by the best doctor in the entire world, that she'll feel better any second now, I realize how much it hurts to love something.

Then I glance over at a man playing with his toy poodle, a lady with a parrot, a guy scratching his mutt's ears; all these people made a choice to care. They didn't have to have pets, they decided they wanted something to love. And one day all these animals will leave them, and it'll be horrible . . . but what they have now is worth it.

When Rosie calls Eve's name, all three of us troop into the examining room. When she comes in, Liz seems surprised. Looking at the carrier, she asks, "Who do we have here?"

"Tatiana." Eve puts the carrier up on the table but doesn't let it go. "She's . . . you can make her better, right?"

"Let's have a look." Liz lets Tat out of the carrier. She is definitely woozy. Liz asks the usual questions about water and heat. Then she feels around Tat's stomach. "How long have you had her?" she asks Eve.

Eve's too upset to think in numbers, so I say, "About seven months."

"Okay." Liz nods. "Do you know if she's been fixed?"

"Fixed?" Eve says blankly.

"If she can have kittens," says Liz.

Eve's eyes widen. "Oh, my God. Is that it? Is she going to be a . . . mom?"

Liz smiles. "Let's run some tests."

"Guys, I don't know if Tat's cut out for motherhood," says Eve as we wait for the test results at Anna's house.

"They'd be beautiful," says Anna, petting Tat's fur.

"Yeah, but she's such a princess. The whole diaper, feeding, birth thing . . ."

I laugh. "She's not going to change diapers."

"Well, you know what I mean." She picks Tat up, holds her nose to nose. "Who's the daddy? Can you tell me that? Whoever he is, we'll track him down, make sure he doesn't walk out on you."

"Yeah," says Anna. "That's a good question. Who—?"

Just then Mouli comes padding into the room. Anna freezes. Noticing she's stopped talking, Eve says, "What?" Then looks where she's looking.

"Oh. No," she says.

"Well, I don't think it could be Beesley," I say slowly. "He was too old."

"But that tub of lard?" Eve squeals, pointing her chin toward Mouli.

"Hey!" says Anna, offended.

"Well, sorry, but let's face it, we're talking beauty and the beast here."

Anna gathers her cat in her arms. "Mouli is just as much a star as Tat. Only in a different way."

"Yeah," says Eve sarcastically. "The obnoxious, thuggy, big orange thing way."

Anna narrows her eyes, breathes through her nose. Sensing possible violence, I say, "Okay, guys . . ."

Thank God, the phone rings. Anna goes to get it. We listen as she says, "Hello?" She nods at us, to say it's the clinic. "Okay. O . . . kay. Great. So, what do we do in the meantime?" She starts taking down notes. "All right, thanks. Thanks a lot."

She hangs up the phone. Eve says, "So?"

"We're going to be grandparents."

I look at Tat and Mouli. "These are going to be some potent kittens."

By the time I get home, it's almost dinnertime. My mom has gone out to dinner with Liz. So I make myself a hummus sandwich and read my favorite James Herriot book for the ninety millionth time.

It's weird, but the main thing I notice now that my dad's not here? The silence. When I come home, I don't hear the piano through the front door. I don't hear it as I fall asleep. I don't hear my dad interrupt his own playing with instructions, "No—ah, yes." Even the creak of our old piano bench, the flap of pages turning, the thud of the piano closing.

And I miss it.

Going back to my room, I pass by the living room and take a peek at the piano. It looks alone, standing there in the corner, shut up and quiet. Also proud, like it knows I feel bad for it and doesn't want my pity. A piano exists to make music—but it can only do that with the help of someone else. Must be hard to not have that someone. . . .

Sitting down on the bench, I push back the cover. I haven't practiced in so long; the stretch of keys feels endless. I don't know where to put my hands, feel afraid of making the wrong sounds. Instruments are so delicate, they don't need someone stupid pounding away on them without knowing what they're doing.

I shut the piano.

Then open it.

Carefully, I put one finger on a key and press. The

sound, low and strong, fills the empty room. It sounds sad, mournful. But right. The house needed to hear that sound. It was in the air, but no one was paying attention.

Lifting my hand, I play another note to keep it company. This one's higher, lighter, still sad, but not so final. Then I feel confused and stop. I can't do this. Not on my own.

The Schumann sheet music is still on the stand. I remember how I never open the music to a new piece until my dad starts the lesson.

But my dad's not here. And I want to play this piece.

I open the book, scan the first line. Then, putting my fingers on the keys, I begin.

THIRTEEN

DEATH

Transformation, clearing away the old to make way for the new

When I was little, I hated hide-and-seek. Whenever someone yelled "Ready or not, here I come!" I always thought, *Rats, I should've hidden better. They'll find me in five seconds.* I spent the whole time dreading the moment when I'd feel that tap. It always felt like a slap. *Ha-ha, found you!*

I am not ready for my dad to be home. But he's coming. Ready or not.

It's been three weeks, and the clinic says he can leave. My mom says he's much better. But I don't know what that means.

This morning when she asked if I wanted to come with her to pick him up, I said no. I know I should have said yes, but I just couldn't. My mom said that was okay, they'd be back by lunch.

I really don't know how this is supposed to work. I assume my dad would like to still be drinking. Only, now he has to do what we say, if he wants to be around us. I don't see how this is a good thing. How it makes anyone happier. It's not like he's changed. He's just pretending. I remember my first card, the Seven of Cups, the one that warned me about fantasies and wishful thinking. I'm worried that's what we're all doing: deciding my dad will be okay because—well, he has to be, right? Otherwise . . .

I look through the stuff I printed out at the library. It says you have to "detach," like, not freak out over everything the alcoholic does. Which says to me, basically not care.

It's almost one when the door opens and I hear my dad's voice in the house: "Hello?"

I wait for a moment, then go out into the hall. My dad's standing at the door, all the way at the other end. I say, "Hey, Dad."

He stretches his arms out, gives me a half smile, like he's not sure I'll come or not.

My mom says, "Syd, why don't you make us some tea?" I nod, go into the kitchen.

Here's what my dad looks like: smaller.

At dinner my dad drinks diet soda. For some reason, it bothers me. Like, *See what a good boy I'm being? I'm drinking DIET SODA.*

He tells stories about the clinic. He talks about his doctor, how it turned out they were both big Mets fans and how they totally agreed on everything. He makes it sound like they were friends. Like everyone else might have been there because they had a problem with alcohol, but my dad was there so this doctor would have someone interesting to talk to.

That night when I go to the bathroom, I hear my mom tell him, "Give it time. It'll work out."

I can tell: "It" is me. I am what's supposed to work out.

And every day, I feel it: the expectation. Is it working out? When will Syd get over it? Every day, I feel watched. Is she in a good mood? A bad mood? Ready to forget? Isn't she over that cat by now?

I tell myself I am lucky. The cards were right, but not in the way I thought. My dad is still alive. The worst has not happened. But that doesn't mean something hasn't died.

Since we don't know exactly when she got pregnant, we can't be sure when Tat's kittens will arrive. But Liz says it'll definitely be before school starts in September, which is good because I think Eve would refuse to go to school if it meant leaving Tat. Anna and I are on red alert. When we get the call, we are to head to Eve's immediately, bringing Mouli, as the father must be present at the birth. All family visits must be canceled. No visits to malls more than two hours away. And no long phone calls, so the line will be free.

A week after my dad comes home, I stop by Liz's office to ask how we'll know when to bring Tat in. Puzzled, she smiles and says, "You don't bring her in, honey. Tat knows what to do. She just needs a little help."

Nervous, I say, "From you."

Washing her hands, Liz says, "I think you're more than qualified."

"*Me?*"

"Yeah, you. You've got all those books. Time to put them to good use." She switches off the water, dries her hands. "How's your dad doing?"

"Okay, I guess."

"Is he playing?" I shake my head. "Are you playing?"

I was, but not since my dad came home. If he hears me practice, I know he'll want to help. And I'm not ready for that yet.

I don't know how to even begin to be ready for

Tat's labor. I start reading the second I get home, but the more I read, the more nervous I get. It all seems like meaningless steps and procedures, nothing to do with the messy business of life coming into the world.

This is the biggest thing I've ever done—literally, a matter of life and death—and the "What ifs" are pounding in my head. What if there are problems? What if Tat can't handle it? What if I can't handle it—and one of the kittens or even Tat dies? Who says the Death card covers only one death?

I spend my mornings at the library. Every once in a while, I wander through the stacks, hoping to run into Mark. I never do. Occasionally, I have a fantasy of delivering the kittens with such skill that Mark falls madly in love with me. I imagine him saying, *Wow, you really are a lion tamer.* Then I give myself a good hard pinch for being such a dork.

One day I come home and I can hear the TV. My dad must be watching some baseball game. He watches a lot of sports these days. As I pass by, he says, "You've had two calls, both from Eve, neither of which I understood. One was 'Red alert! Red alert!' The second was 'False alarm! False alarm!' Does this make sense to you?"

I nod. "Her cat's going to have kittens." That seems a little short, so I add, "She's freaking out."

"Ah. That's unusual for Eve."

There was a time when my dad could joke about Eve like that and I'd laugh. Now I feel protective of her, like, *Who are you to judge?*

Then he takes something off the piano. "By the way, I found this."

It's the brochure Mr. Courtney sent me. Embarrassed, I'm about to say, *I meant to throw that out,* when my dad says, "This guy Courtney doesn't hear no, does he?"

Which annoys me as well. "He sent it to be nice," I say.

"Uh-huh." My dad tosses the brochure on the piano. But he throws too hard, and it slides to the floor.

"Don't throw that," I tell him. "I might want it."

"Why?"

"I might want to go," I say wildly.

"You don't want that, baby, believe me." My dad sounds almost like his old self when he says this. There's a little warning in his voice, almost like a threat. Like, *You better be careful, Sydney. Something bad might happen to you if you don't listen to me.* And I realize, that doesn't sit right with me anymore.

"Who says?" My dad stares at me. "Seriously. Who says?" Because I don't think my dad has ever said out loud that he doesn't think I can handle things. I want him to at least have the guts to say it.

When he doesn't answer, I pick the brochure up from the floor. Standing on the other side of the piano, I say, "You know what the big problem with Julliard is? Maybe the big problem is, *you* couldn't handle it."

I expect yelling, but it doesn't come. In his silence my voice rises. "But maybe I can. Maybe I'm tired of feeling scared all the time. Maybe I don't want to be frightened of people anymore. Maybe I want to try things so I can find out if I can handle them or not. Maybe . . ."

I'm about to say, *Maybe I don't want to be you, Dad. Once it was the only thing in the world I wanted: to be just like you. Now? Forget it.*

When the phone rings, we both stand there for a moment, not sure what to do. Do we answer? Let it go? Then, going to the kitchen, I snatch up the phone. "Hello?"

"RED ALERT! RED ALERT!"

When Anna and I arrive, Eve yanks open the door. Her hair is even spikier than usual, her eyes are wild, and she's wearing her pajama top over her favorite pair of destroyed jeans.

"Oh, my God," she says. "Tat's freaking out, guys."

We hurry back to Eve's room, where Tat is panting,

pacing, yowling. But it's all totally normal, and I tell Eve so.

"That's what Liz said when I called her, but she looks like she's in pain. What if they can't come out? Syd, could you call Liz? She'll come over if you ask her."

Tat races to the corner and pukes. "Oh, God," says Anna.

Someone has to stay calm, so I say, "Okay, guys, Tat doesn't need us freaking out too. This is what's supposed to happen during the first stage of labor. Any second now, she's going to get on her bed and chill out. That's the second stage."

"What's the third?" asks a nervous Anna, who's looking a little sick.

Lots of gross stuff and blood, I think. "Kittens," I say brightly. Mouli thumps angrily inside his carrier. Tat screams. Eve claps her hands to her ears. I tell Anna to take Mouli somewhere else.

"Where?"

"Anywhere." I turn to Eve. "Do you have any old towels?" She nods. "Go and get them." Eve races off, which leaves me alone with Tat. I look at her, panting miserably, totally freaked by what's going on in her body. Normally, she's such a proud creature, like she'd never need sympathy from a mere human. But today she's utterly vulnerable.

I say, "I'm sorry, sweetie, I know it hurts. You'll get through this, I promise." *You and me both,* I think. But actually, now that I'm in it, I feel much less anxious. Getting Tat through this safe is all that matters.

Eve returns with towels. They're white and look brand new. "Eve, these are going to get messy. You're sure your parents won't mind?"

"I'm not having Tat give birth on scruffy old rags," she says.

Deciding that it's Eve's problem, I take the towels and arrange them like a nest around Tat's bed. Looking at the list I made, I say, "Now I need scissors, petroleum jelly, disinfectant, a heating pad, and dental floss."

"Dental floss?"

"Yep." Best not to tell Eve why at this point.

Anna returns—without Mouli. "I found a place for him," she gasps. "How's she doing?"

"Just fine," I say firmly. "Right. Now—we wait."

And wait we do. For an hour and a half. Convinced something is horribly wrong, Eve is shoving the phone into my hand and demanding I call Liz when Tat clambers up on her nest and starts purring. Eve breaks into smiles. "Whoa, just like you said."

"Way to go, Tat," says Anna.

"What now?" asks Eve.

"More waiting," I tell her. "This is Tat's job, we're only here for support." Eve and Anna sit back down. Tat goes rigid, her legs stretching as far as they'll go. "Just a contraction," I tell them.

"I'm never doing this," says Eve. "Just for the record, I am never, ever doing this."

"I'd do it," says Anna. "But you guys have to be there."

Tat goes stiff again. In a shaky voice Anna says, "Guys, something totally disgusting just came out of her."

"That's the placenta," I say. The towels are officially destroyed. "Next up—kittens."

But for a while there's no sign of kittens. Tat strains and pushes for forty minutes, but no babies. What I don't tell Anna and Eve is that if Tat goes for an entire hour like this without giving birth, then we do have to call Liz because she's in trouble. For the next fifteen minutes I keep a close eye on my watch—and a closer eye on Tat, hoping, praying a kitten emerges.

"Is this taking too long?" whispers Eve.

"I think we're fine," I say, trying to keep my voice calm.

I am just trying to figure out how to call Liz without throwing Eve into a total panic when Tat screams and gives a huge heave. A slimy bubblelike thing appears.

Another heave, and it pops out onto the towel. Anna leaps up. "Oh, my God!"

"She did it!" yells Eve.

Immediately, Tat starts licking at her newborn, breaking the amniotic sac and cleaning it off, which is great, because if she didn't, I was going to have to do it. As it is, there's one thing I do have to do—and I'm really nervous about it. Taking a deep breath, I hold out my hand and say, "Dental floss."

Eve slaps it into my hand. "What—you're going to clean his teeth?"

"Nope," I say, picking up the scissors. Going over to Tat, I see she's already trying to cut the umbilical cord herself. Gently pushing her head away, I tie the cord tightly with a piece of floss. Then I take a deep breath. I have never cut a living thing before, and even though I know Tat will just chew through the cord if I don't, it still makes me queasy.

Okay, I tell myself. *Okay . . .* And I snip.

Behind me, Anna says, "Syd, you are like, Pioneer Woman. I am in awe."

Crouching down by the nest, Eve says, "God, look at him—her? It's like . . . tiny."

Anna kneels. "Hi, little guy. Welcome to the world."

For a second I look at the kitten woozily squirming, and my heart melts. Then I say, "Guys, we should give her some room. Number two should be coming any minute."

Over the next few hours number two comes. Then number three. Numbers four and five arrive just around suppertime. Eve immediately starts coming up with names for them, until I point out she has no idea if they're boys or girls.

"Oh, don't be a gender fascist," she says.

Anna is sitting cross-legged on the floor, staring at the nest. "Wow . . . ," she says. "Wow."

Which pretty much covers it. It's so weird to think that yesterday none of these kittens existed. Now there are five new lives in the world, bumping around, making themselves felt, ready to cause all kinds of trouble and give all kinds of love. I think about who might get them. An old lady who doesn't have anyone, a shy kid who needs a friend, some businessman who might work less hard if he had someone to come home to. All these new connections. All this . . . life.

"I want to keep them all," says Eve.

"Your parents will kill you," says Anna reasonably.

Just then we hear another scream—not Tat. This one is human and definitely male. It's followed by a cat scream, also not from Tat. Which means it could only come from . . .

"Anna," I ask, "where'd you put Mouli?"

Nervous, she glances at Eve. "You said Mark wasn't home."

I leap up. "You put him in Mark's room?"

Eve giggles. "Excellent."

Another yell, another yowl—louder this time. We run out into the hall to find Mark in the bathroom, standing on the toilet. Mouli is prowling the bathroom floor, fat paws slapping the tiles. At the sight of Mark, I feel a horrible urge to laugh. He looks so cute clinging to the shower curtain.

"It's just a cat," Eve taunts.

"It is not just a cat," says Mark. "It is a feline wrecking machine. Go look in my room—go *look*! He's totally deranged."

As Eve goes to check out the damage, Anna tries to grab Mouli, but Mouli is in no mood to be grabbed. He lashes out at her and races for the door. Anna beats him to it, shutting the door behind her in her desperation to get away from his claws.

Which leaves just me, Mark, and Mouli in the bathroom. Mark puts his hand on the wall and leans against it. "So—how are you?"

I cannot smile. I cannot laugh. Nothing about this is funny. Poor Mark is trapped. Mouli is looking to hunt, kill, destroy. And I . . .

. . . know nothing can happen with Mark, so this is not a big deal.

As calmly as possible, I say, "Fine. I'm . . . fine."

"Good. I'm glad you're fine."

"I am."

"Good." He points at Mouli. "This cat is insane."

"He's . . . a little crazy."

"You admit that?"

I watch Mouli start shredding one of Mrs. Baylor's towels—this poor woman is going to be towelless. "Kind of hard not to."

"I've never heard you say something like that about an animal."

"What do you mean?"

"No, just . . . it's always four legs good, two legs bad with you."

Annoyed, I say, "That is not true."

"You said you can trust animals but that people are a whole different thing."

"Yeah and . . ." I'm about to say, *And didn't this summer prove me right? I trusted my dad, I trusted you—and look where it got me.*

But the fact is, not trusting people hasn't gotten me anywhere great either.

Then Mark says, "You said we were going to talk later."

Bristling, I say, "And you said, 'Yeah.'"

"So?"

"So?"

"So," I say, stating the utterly obvious, "you didn't call."

"Because *you* said we would talk. That meant *you* would call."

"Why would I call when I knew you didn't want to hear from me?"

"Why would you know something that's completely not true?"

Okay, this is ridiculous. Because clearly, it was up to Mark to call. He is the guy, he is older, he kissed me—he's got the power. The one with the power calls. They don't make the one without power completely embarrass herself. Besides, I called him first.

"Look," I tell him, "I didn't call you because I didn't want you to feel like you had to make me feel better or anything." He looks confused. "You know, like when you kissed me. You only did it because you felt sorry for me. Like, 'Oh, poor little Syd, her cat's dead, her family's screwed up . . .'"

"I didn't feel sorry for you, I felt sorry for me."

"Why?"

"'Cause . . ." Mark gives the shower curtains an angry shake. "'Cause I liked you, you dingbat. I don't like *anybody*. I made a total fool of myself."

"You did not. *I* did."

"How?"

"By liking *you,* you big dope. By having this ridiculous, ginormous crush—"

"On me?"

"Who else, Mouli?"

Mark considers this. "You had a crush on me?"

I throw a roll of toilet paper at him. "Yes, duh. And you knew it. So when you felt sorry for me, you were like, 'Well, I guess I can kiss her, make her feel better . . .'"

"That was the hardest thing I've ever done. Reaching the last level of Halo was not nearly as hard."

I roll my eyes. "Gee, thanks."

Mark pounds the wall. "God, you know—pretty girls don't have a clue how hard it is for a guy to talk to you, let alone make a move."

Pretty? Mark thinks I'm pretty? If there's one word I thought Mark associated with me, it was "kid." A baby. Eve's little friend. But . . . pretty?

I look at Mark standing on the toilet, crumpling the shower curtain in his fist. And I realize: I make Mark shy. All this time that I've been shy around him, he's been shy around me. Because—and maybe it's because he doesn't have the best eyesight in the world—he thinks I'm pretty.

I may have finally met the man who is a bigger chicken than I am.

Now Mouli is standing right in front of the toilet, tail twitching. Mark asks, "Is this where he pounces and rips my face off?"

I don't think so, but with Mouli, you can never tell. Crouching, I make puss-puss noises, trying to get Mouli's attention. His tail twitches more violently, but he doesn't turn around.

"Mouli," I whisper, "don't you want to see your kids? They're so cute, Mouli, you're just going to love them."

Mark says, "Syd, really, you should get my dad. This cat's scary."

Mouli is being scary right now, but Mark's dad isn't going to know how to handle him. Anna would know, but I can't risk leaving Mark and Mouli together in a small bathroom. And if I yell for her, Mouli might be startled and pounce.

"Mouli, Mouli, Mouli . . . ," I say, making a song out of it. "Mouli Man, come on over, Mouli Man. You are definitely master of your domain. No need to keep bullying people."

Mouli glances over his shoulder. "Come on, Mouli. You've got so many better things to do than shred defenseless humans. For the sake of your newborn kittens, show mercy."

"Oh, now he's a medieval knight," says Mark.

"Shh. I'm just trying to calm him down."

And it's working. Mouli takes one step around, then another. Now he's standing sideways, looking back and forth between me and Mark. In his head it's, *Shred . . . show mercy? Shred . . . show mercy?*

And I guess he chooses mercy, because he comes padding over to me. Gently, I pick him up and say to Mark, "You can come down now."

"When he's on the other side of the door," Mark says.

With Tat so tired and the kittens so new, it's best to keep everyone quiet, so I put Mouli back in his carrier. When I go back to the bathroom, Mark is sitting on the toilet, chin on fist, looking bothered. I trace the bathroom tile with the tip of my sandal. My courage is fading in the silence when Mark says, "Did you really have a crush on me?"

"You want me to say it again?"

"Yeah."

I sigh. "I had a crush on you."

"What about now?"

"What do you mean?"

"You could be thinking, 'Um, kiss . . . kind of like dead fish.' I could have killed the crush."

"You didn't kill the crush."

Mark stands up. "I didn't?"

"No." There's no point in denying it anymore.

Mark takes a step forward. "So, if I tried to kiss you again, you wouldn't run screaming in terror?"

"Probably not."

Mark hesitates. "Probably . . ."

I remember what Anna said about geeks: Often, you have to make the first move. So, taking a deep breath, I go up to Mark, grab his face, and put my mouth on his. Almost like a slap of hands, but with mouths.

All of a sudden, Mark is kissing me back. After a few tries we figure out how to both kiss at the same time—which really is best, in case anyone was wondering.

Then, behind me, I hear, "No, no, no, no, no . . . NO!"

I break off, turn around to see Eve at the door, eyes shut, hand over her heart. She moans, "Air, I can't get any air."

Mark rolls his eyes. "And the award for worst actress goes to . . ."

Eve glares. "Shut up, perv." She turns to me. "Syd, you're tired. You just delivered five kittens and you don't know what you're doing. I understand, and we don't have to talk about it ever again."

Mark says, "Eve . . ."

But this is my fight. I say, "Eve, I hate to break it to you, but we might have to talk about it again."

"No. Really. We don't."

"No. Really. We do. Because this is happening. And you and I are going to stay friends anyway."

I have never stood up to Eve. I know me being with Mark will bug her, but I also know that won't stop it from happening.

Eve chews her lip, glances from me to Mark and back again. "What if you guys break up? What if you hate each other? Like, whose side do I take?"

I think about breaking up with Mark—how horrible that would be. And how I'd die if she took Mark's side and she hated me and we weren't friends. And where would Anna be in all of this? Maybe Mark and I shouldn't go out, it'd just get too crazy.

Then I shake myself. Everything I'm thinking about is way, way in the future. And who knows what will happen? Not even the cards can see that far ahead.

Well, I think, *they did see some things.* They saw separation and alienation. They saw anxiety. And a journey. They saw illness . . . and a death.

But they didn't see that I could go through all that stuff and be okay. How could they? I sure didn't.

And if you can go through horrible stuff and still be okay, if there just aren't that many things that are the great disaster, hurtling at you like a meteor, then . . . why worry about it?

I give Eve a hug and say, "We can't live on what if. We just have to do what is."

Mother and kittens seem to be doing well, so Anna and I decide to go. Anna is quiet all the way home. When I ask if she's okay, she says, "Yeah, just tired."

As we go up in the elevator, Anna says, "Oh—hey." She fumbles with her bag. "There's something I wanted to give you. In honor of the kittens."

"You don't have to . . ."

"No, I do." She hands me a folded piece of paper as the elevator bounces to a stop at her floor. Getting out, she says, "Just . . . read that when you get home, okay?" She waves quickly, then the door shuts.

Looking at the paper, I'm totally mystified. Is it a letter? A picture of Beesley? I open it almost without thinking. It's a photocopy of a page from Anna's tarot book.

The Death card page, to be exact.

I almost crumple it up; I've had enough of death and endings and sadness. I don't want any more. But then I notice that Anna's highlighted some of the lines. Leaning against the wall, I read: *Death: Loss. Transformation. Clearing away the old to make way for the new. Illness. The end of a familiar situation. A new era.*

I have to read it again to make sure Anna didn't somehow write in all the happy words. But the old, crumbly print is the same. The card's picture of Death—that nasty smiling skeleton—is the same as it is in the book.

Only, it's not nearly as bad as I thought. There's definitely sadness and loss. But there's newness, too. Yes, Beesley died—but now there are all those new squirming kittens. Maybe Beesley had to leave the world to make room for them.

As for transformation . . . God, in the last six hours I have yelled at my dad, delivered kittens, faced down Mouli, kissed a boy, and fought with Eve. I should feel exhausted. Instead, I feel giddy, like, *Whoo-hoo, what's next?*

Getting out of the elevator, I go to the front door. Through the door, I hear something—the faint sound of the piano. It can only be my dad. Yet it doesn't sound like him. My dad goes for big, bold sounds; there's lots of drama and excitement in his playing. This is quiet, hesitant playing, like he's just learning.

Curious, I go into the living room. My dad looks up.

I say, "Keep going."

But he doesn't. Instead, he takes something off the top of the piano, holds it out to me. It's the pamphlet, with the application completely filled out.

"Just needs your signature," he says.

I look at it, think how funny it would be if I sent it and didn't get in. Or what if I did get in, but it's way too hard? What if . . . ?

Then I feel my dad take my hand, his fingers lacing through mine. He says, "I never thought you didn't have the talent."

"I know."

"But I told myself I didn't want that pressure for you. I told myself that your path was to be a veterinarian, that I shouldn't push you into my life. Because"— he looks up at me—"kids shouldn't be pushed."

I remember that picture, my dad as a baby with his hands on the piano. And the card that talked about difficulties and the inability to launch. At the time I wondered why images from my dad's childhood turned up in my reading. Now I know.

Then my dad says, "But they shouldn't be frightened, either. And they shouldn't be held back because . . ."—he hesitates—". . . because that would show their old man that there was nothing wrong with Julliard, he just couldn't hack it."

It hurts so hard to hear my dad admit this. "I bet he could—he decided not to."

He waves his hand dismissively. "Your whole life,

I've been telling you other people are stronger than you. By telling you not to compete, I told you you couldn't. And that was dead wrong. If you want this"—he taps the brochure—"I'm right behind you. I'll help you prep for the audition . . . if you want."

He sounds uncertain, like his help is the last thing I'd want. For a moment I want my old dad back. I want it to be me and him against the crummy world. I want to know that I am a vet-to-be, not a musician-to-be, that I have no real talent, that my choices are limited. I want everything to be simple, even if it's not true.

This is all new territory. But isn't that what the Death card promises? The end of a familiar situation?

Without speaking, I go and sit down on the bench next to my dad. He puts his arm around me, leans his head on mine. And for a little while we just sit there like that.

Then he says, "Hey, how many kittens?"

"Five."

"So . . . might we be having an addition to the family?"

My mind goes to the second and last kittens born. The second one squinched his eyes up when he yawned in a way that said, *Man, where have I landed?* And the last one was . . . last. Easy to forget. So, of course, I want her.

I say, "I'd have to ask Eve."

"So ask."

"Okay. Hey, Dad?"

"Yes, baby?"

"Maybe if I went to Julliard, you could come with me." I grin. "Start over."

He laughs at this, a real laugh, the first one I've heard from him in a long, long time. He laughs so hard, he has to wipe his eyes. Finally, he says, "No, honey, you can't go back. Just forward to whatever the future holds."

"Do you think you'll go back to teaching?"

"I don't know. I'm sorry, honey, I don't know anything right now. And I don't want to make too many promises, because the ones I make I have to keep."

Looking at the river of black and white in front of us, I remember that this was supposed to be the summer my dad taught me Schumann. But it turned into a very different summer. I like that my dad doesn't know what his future holds. When Eve was sure she knew the future, it made her cocky, careless. My dad knows he's creating his future every day.

Without thinking, I put a finger on one of the keys. The thing about "Heart and Soul" is you can start playing it without knowing, just by striking the same note a few times. And because I've played it so many times, I guess my hand goes to that key right away.

My dad laughs a little, starts playing the bass part—*bumpa bumpa, bumpa*. I hit the three notes again, then play the rest of the tune. It feels silly at first—I mean, it's kind of a dumb song. But there's something about playing something you know so well, it's in your hands and you don't even have to think about the notes.

So instead, I think about the first time my dad sat with me at the piano, how he held my hand, made me feel that this never-ending row of notes and chords and keys was something I could master, that I could create something if I was brave enough. This is where he taught me that mistakes don't matter. They will happen if you're working hard, and the only thing to do when you hit that awful wrong note is to forget it, keep going, keep trying.

And someday, if you work hard enough, it'll be whole and good again.

FOURTEEN
SHE WHO WOULD THE FUTURE KNOW...

I wish I could say the cards were right. That Anna got her love, Eve, her fame, and me, whatever it was I asked for. In a weird way, my reading came the most true. There was a loss, there was a death, and there was a change—some of it awful, some of it good. Which adds up to okay, I guess. Actually, when I'm with Mark, a lot better than okay.

But that's me. Eve is still hurting over her audition, but she has the kittens to distract her. Anna's really down, although, being Anna, she doesn't complain. So one afternoon I call her and say, "I have a major need for ice cream."

"I don't need ice cream," she says gloomily. "I've been in mondo pig-out mode."

"Oh, stop. Meet me downstairs in five minutes."

We walk over to Wiffle's, where I get a pumpkin cone and Anna gets raspberry sorbet in a cup. There's a little bench outside, and we sit in the August heat, slowly eating our ice cream.

Trying to get her to talk, I say, "Have you seen the kittens?"

Anna shuts her eyes. "Ugh. Eve's like Ms. Schizo. Every day, it's 'Which one do I keep? Which one do I give away? I can't give any away.'"

"Really? She promised my dad we could have two."

"That's why you're not hearing about it," she says tartly. "That's why I get all the joy. Oh, God, that was nasty, I'm sorry. Ignore me, I'm weird right now."

"What's wrong?"

"Urrrg." She kicks at the pavement as she decides whether or not to spill. "Oh, Nelson's supposed to be back by now, and I haven't heard from him. And, yes, I know it's my fault, because how can I expect him to call when I was so mean to him?" She sighs. "School starts in a week. You have a boyfriend, Eve's got all these kittens, and I'm back to being nice, boring Anna. Except I'm not even nice anymore, I'm a jealous poop."

Frowning, she jabs her spoon into her cup. "This summer has officially sucked."

"Well," I say, trying to think of something to cheer her up, "at least it's almost over."

When we're finished with our ice cream, we head home. Stopping in the lobby, Anna says, "Hold on. I gotta pick up the mail. Russell's waiting for his Humane Society membership." She rolls her eyes. "Free penguin calendar."

"Hey, their penguin calendar rocks," I say jokingly.

Anna pulls the mail out of the box and starts flipping through it. "No calendar . . . Russell's going to be—" Then she stops, holds up one of the envelopes.

"What?"

"Um, it's from Nelson," she says in a small voice.

"Whoa." I take the batch of mail from her, set it on one of the lobby tables. "Do you want me to go away while you read it or . . ."

"No!" She grabs my wrist. "No, definitely stay."

"Okay," I say nervously. Somehow the letter feels like an emotional bomb. Don't people only write letters to deliver bad news, stuff they don't want to say in person or even over the phone?

Taking a deep breath, Anna opens the envelope, takes out a thick wad of folded paper. Whatever the news is, there's a lot of it. I put my arm around her, give her a squeeze as she opens it.

Then I see why there are so many pages. It's not a normal letter, with words and paragraphs. In fact, there aren't that many words at all. Just pictures, drawn in heavy black ink. Over Anna's shoulder, I see a boy and a girl, wearing braids just like the ones I gave Anna when we did her "Get Declan" makeover.

In the first panel the boy is sitting alone at a table with a storm of people moving all around him but ignoring him completely. The occasional face in the crowd looks mean. They're usually laughing at the boy.

Then in the next panel the girl with braids walks by. She has huge eyes and is surrounded by lines that I guess are meant to be light. She's obviously the only thing the boy sees.

The story takes you through everything that happened—Nelson watching as Anna and Declan dance (the next panel shows him with crazy eyes, tearing at his hair, howling, *Nooo!*), then Anna with a sword taking on the principal to get Nelson unsuspended.

"He drew you like Joan of Arc," I say.

The panels about the kiss are adorable, all eyes and mouth, with Nelson floating home in the way goofy cartoons show love. Then we get to the fight. I'm not sure how Nelson will show this; I worry Joan of Arc is suddenly going to go Ninja on him. But instead, he shows Anna talking and himself with his mouth stitched closed with big ugly thread. A thought balloon over his head screams, *Say something! Don't be a jerk! Can—not—speak! Gaaahhh!*

Then Anna walks away and he's alone.

The next panels show Nelson on vacation. The storm of mean, laughing faces is back, he's got dark circles under his eyes, and his mouth is still stitched shut. Then, all of a sudden, he brightens up, the light rays are back. We see him racing around, scribbling, then at a mailbox.

The next-to-last panel is the only one in color. It shows a rose. I guess just like the one Nelson gave Anna, although at the time we thought Declan gave it to her.

The last panel is blank, except for a storm of question marks.

Turning over the last page, Anna says, "I guess . . . I should call him?"

"Yeah," I laugh. "I guess you should."

In the elevator Anna says, "It's so weird. Your reading sort of came true, right?" I nod. "And now it seems like my reading's coming true again, so . . ."

I finish her thought. "So, what about Eve?"

"Right. You know, *Making It!* starts airing next week."

"I know." You can't not know. The hype has been nonstop.

Anna says, "Eve's worried they're going to use her audition as one of the 'Can You Believe This Person Thought She Had Talent?' moments."

I wince. "I can't believe they'd do that. But maybe we should schedule our Farewell to Freedom Day the date it premieres. That way, she won't spend the whole day obsessing."

"*Great* idea. Oops, here's me." We stop on Anna's floor.

I give her a hug, say, "Good luck with Nelson."

Smiling, she narrows her eyes mysteriously. "Is it luck, or is it . . . in the cards?"

"Stop!" I yell, pushing her out the door.

Every summer, before we go back to school, we have a Farewell to Freedom Day. We always think we're going to do something amazing—go to Coney Island or stay the night in a fancy hotel. And yet we always end up shopping, watching movies, and having a sleepover. But as Anna points out, if we didn't like it, we wouldn't keep doing it.

Of the three of us, Eve is always the most bummed.

Every Farewell Day, she says, "I can't *believe* we have to go back," like she was expecting the government to ban school or something. This year is the worst. She told everyone at school she was auditioning. Now she's convinced they'll all be watching tonight and witness her humiliation.

Anna and I have decided we won't mention the show unless Eve does. If she wants to watch tonight, fine. If she wants to pretend it's not happening, also fine.

We start the day with breakfast at Fluff's, and Anna suggests we go to Bloomingdale's. Eve loves Bloomingdale's, it's prime shoplifting territory for her. But now she just shrugs, says, "Whatever."

As we take the bus crosstown, I say, "Can you believe we're starting high school?"

Eve sighs. "Four more years of misery and torture."

Anna gives her a gentle kick. "Hey, Ms. Star of the School Musical, you can't pretend people hate you anymore."

"What if I still hate them?" says Eve.

Thankfully, she cheers up a bit when we get to Bloomies. Nine floors full of stuff, ready for plunder. As we go in, Anna says, "If you get caught, we don't know you."

"I don't get caught," says Eve, striding through the doors.

We wander around the first floor, which is makeup, bags, and jewelry. Eve checks out a bracelet. I hope she "remembers" to put it back.

"Hey, guys?" Anna holds up a bag. "What do you think?"

Watching her model the bag, I remember the shopping trip we made last fall when we were going to transform Anna into the Great Geek Hope of Eberly so she could win over Declan. There has been a transformation. She's still the same great Anna, but being the stage manager for the musical and surviving all that romantic turmoil has given her confidence. She looks happy and excited, the kind of girl any new kid at school wants as their friend. Anna is definitely ready for high school.

Eve inspects the bag. "Nelson'll hate it. You need to go more Goth."

Anna grins. "Nelson doesn't care about stuff like that." She wrinkles her nose happily. "I love that about him."

Eve goes quiet. She even puts back the bracelet.

While Anna buys the bag, I say to Eve, "Anna'll be cool about the boyfriend thing."

Eve sticks her finger in some eyeliner, smears it on

the counter. "Yeah, yeah." Then she looks at me. "I know I've been a turd about you and Mark."

Oh. My. God. Is Eve actually admitting she might have been wrong? Wanting to give her room to be honest, I say, "It is weird . . ."

Eve picks up a lipstick, brings it to her pocket, then puts it back. In a rush she says, "The thing is, Mark's good at everything. The whole school thing, the good son routine. I know he's going to be married and have kids and have the perfect house and some great job that my parents can brag about. But I figured at least Mark would be boring. And he'd be with somebody boring. Not *you*. Not, like, one of the two best people in the universe."

"Three," I say, hugging her. "There are three best."

Eve's mouth quirks up in a thank-you. Then she says sadly, "Also, I used to think, 'Well, okay, I'll be famous and I won't care what Mark does.' But doesn't look like that's happening."

I want to tell Eve that the cards were right, that someday she'll have everything she wants. But I can't. Because I don't know. And weirdly, even if she were the most famous person in the world, I think she'd still be bugged that Mark gets all this praise from their parents.

Then Eve bursts out with, "Uck, I *hate* that stupid

show. I can't stop thinking about it."

Hearing her, Anna comes over and asks outright, "Eve, do you want to watch?"

"Are you kidding?" says Eve. "No way."

"But you might be on," I say.

"Yes, exactly," says Eve. "No, thank you. Come on, let's check out watches."

Last year I had the sleepover at my house. The year before was at Anna's, so this time we're at Eve's. Mark is at his friend Chet's. Eve's parents are having dinner with some neighbors. Part of me wonders if they all decided to get out of the house because the show is on.

It's hard not to rush over to the kittens first thing, but when Eve says, "Oh, go and see," I head directly to the blanket nest. Tat is regally licking her paw, ignoring all these kittens squirming around her. I pick out my guys from the pack. I named the girl Begonia, because I wanted a "B" name in memory of Beesley. My dad named the boy Shlomo. Begonia has proud, pointed ears; she looks like a sweet little bat. Shlomo is a baby Mouli, orange and fat pawed. But he's a goofy, happy boy with none of his dad's temper. I cuddle them for a little while, let them crawl around in my lap. I can't wait to take them home.

"Where are the others going?" Anna asks.

"We're keeping her." Eve holds up a sleepily blinking fluff ball with crazy stripes. "I'm calling her Sally. And Yvonne is taking the other two." She sets Sally down. "I'm starved. Let's order."

As Anna calls Chez Wong, I glance at the clock. It's seven thirty. The show starts at eight. But Eve hasn't shown any sign of changing her mind.

But at two minutes to eight, just as Anna is setting out the plastic plates and chopsticks, Eve says, "Oh, I guess we might as well . . . ," and switches on the TV.

We settle in on the floor and open up food cartons. I'm not sure what's the right thing to do: Rag on the show every chance I get? Make fun of the contestants? Or just keep my mouth shut? What if Eve is on, and she's terrible? What if I see exactly why they didn't pick her?

Eve's hands are clenched in her lap. To reassure her, I say, "They might not even show you."

"That's what I'm hoping," she says, not taking her eyes off the set.

As the intro music plays, Anna says, "Cheesy opening." When Peter McElroy appears, we boo and throw wadded-up napkins at the screen. The first one on is a hip-hop dancer from Arkansas, a complete dork who weighs ninety pounds and is, as Eve puts it, "rhythm challenged."

The judges are brutal. And they're even nastier to the next kid, a girl who twirls a baton. I remember what my dad said about people making money off of destroying their love for something. He was right. I am so glad Eve didn't get on this show.

The next girl is a dancer. She can actually dance. The judges all act relieved that—finally!—they've found some sign of talent in the universe. She is good, but frankly, I can't imagine she's better than Eve.

At the commercial Eve says, "I don't think they're going to show me."

"No," says Anna. "They're mostly showing the really awful ones as jokes."

Eve chews on an egg roll, still not sure if she'll be one of those people or not. I tug on one of her spikes to make her smile.

The next selection of contestants is pretty bad too. One or two decent kids, but no one who seems better than Eve. More and more, I wonder: *Why didn't they pick her?*

Then, all of a sudden, they cut to commercial with "When we come back, the voice heard round the world!" And there's Eve on the screen, belting her heart out.

Eve leaps up. "Oh, God. Turn it off, turn it off!"

Anna tries to snatch one of Eve's arms. "You can do this."

Pacing frantically around the room, Eve says, "I'm going to be sick. Did you see me? I'm telling you, turn it off!"

"You looked great. Calm down," I tell her.

"Everyone at school is going to see this," Eve whispers. "They're all going to see me bomb and go, 'Ha-ha. What'd she expect? Loser.'"

The show comes back on in a blare of bad theme music. Caught, unable to run, Eve flops back down on the floor. Anna and I move closer, so we're like bookends on either side.

Eve isn't the first one up. We have to suffer through a girl who believes she's an opera singer. I wince as she screeches her first note, then think, *Stop, she's trying*.

Then the announcer says, "Next, a very little lady with a very big voice . . . ," and Eve saunters into the audition room. She's so happy and confident, I hurt for her.

"I can't watch," Eve moans, and buries her eyes in the crook of her arm. But then she peeps over her elbow.

Peter McElroy asks, "What are you going to perform for us today?" and Eve says, "'Don't Tell Mama' from *Cabaret*."

"An oldie," crows one of the other judges. I throw a napkin at him.

Told to start, Eve clears her throat. The camera

moves in close on her. To me, she just leaps off the screen. I don't understand how the judges don't see it. She's a hundred times more electric than anyone we've seen. When she sings, the judges raise eyebrows and sit back like they're blown away by the force. They exchange looks like, *What is this?* I want to scream, *It's a real voice, you idiots!*

When Eve's done, she looks hopefully at the judges. Knowing what's coming, I take hold of her hand. Anna takes the other one.

"That's a lot of power," says the pop-star judge. "Maybe too much?" *Yeah,* I think, *because all you've got is a squeak.*

"Nuclear," agrees the songwriter. "My eyebrows got singed. By the way, interesting hair."

For "interesting," read weird, I think. *What a jerk.*

On screen, sensing the other two don't like her, Eve glances at Peter McElroy, waiting for him to defend her. He gives her a long look, then says, "I'm very torn about you, Eve. On the one hand, I do think you have talent . . ."

"See," whispers Anna.

"But, to be frank, my colleagues are right: The package needs some . . . polish."

I say, "Package?"

"Lose the spikes, tone down the overall look,"

McElroy suggests. "Get some control of that voice; you've got it on high volume all the time. Study some of the people who have actually made it on the pop scene. Learn from them. I think you'll be back, but right now I'm afraid that for me, it's a no."

As the other two judges echo "No," the camera moves in to capture the look of shock on Eve's face.

Anna yells at the screen. "God, that was such a rip! Mr. Tough Guy totally caved to the other two."

"You were good," I say. "I mean, really good. They turned you down because you weren't . . ."

"Like everybody else," fumes Anna.

"I think he knew that you have talent," I say, "but that you weren't right for the show. I mean . . . it is a pretty cheeseball program."

Hanging her head, Eve swirls a fork around the bottom of a noodle carton. "Come on, guys. They thought I was a freak."

What would my dad say if he were here? I try to remember Eve's reading. It promised her the World. To Eve, that means the world applauding her. The card does promise admiration from others, but it also promises attachment, fulfillment, ultimate change. I look at Tat sleeping with her kittens, think how much Eve, who says she doesn't care about anybody, cares for her. I remember how Eve gave up her anger to be there for me when my dad fell apart. And I remember Eve's face when she walked into that audition room, how focused and powerful she was. Anna and I aren't the only ones who've had a transformation.

I say, "Eve, I think you were amazing."

"Absolutely amazing," says Anna, still fuming.

"But if you want to be famous, you're going to have to learn not to care what people think."

Eve stares at me. "What people think is the whole point. They're the audience."

"But you're the artist," I remind her. "Peter McElroy is not the voice of destiny."

"Well, who is, then?"

Remembering how Eve sounded when she started to sing, so bold and strong, I say, "You are."

Eve's mouth jumps in a half smile as she thinks about this. Finally, she says, "The show does kind of suck."

When the show is over, we get out our blankets and sleeping bags and turn off the lights. In the darkness Eve says, "So, I don't know. Do the cards work, or are they totally bogus?"

There's a long silence. Then Anna says, "Well, it has been a pretty extreme year. Look at everything that's happened since Mrs. Rosemont died. I got Declan . . ."

"Then lost Declan," says Eve.

"Got Nelson," I say.

"Lost Nelson," admits Anna.

"Got Nelson again," I say.

"Okay," says Eve. "So the Lovers card was right for Anna. What about you, Syd? Your dad didn't die."

"The cards never said he would," says Anna. "They just said there would be change and that the change would involve loss."

I hesitate. I didn't lose my dad and I did. I don't think he's a god anymore—but I think that's a good thing. What he'll be in the future, I don't know. But I guess that's why change is scary—you don't know. And I guess that's why people love the cards. They think if they know in advance, they can control things. Like Eve said, at least you feel prepared.

But that's an illusion. There's no way I could have been prepared for the way I lost Beesley. And there's no way I could have been prepared for Mark, either. So what did "knowing" get me?

On the other hand, when I think of how clueless I was, how I thought my dad was just fine—or would be, if people like my mom would just leave him alone— I'm glad that I know better now. The cards showed me I have to look closer, even if reality isn't always clear. They showed me that I have to ask the questions, even if the answers are scary. And they showed me that sometimes the thing you're most afraid of can be the best thing that ever happens to you. That's definitely worth knowing.

"Well, my reading didn't come true, I can tell you that," grumps Eve.

"But, Eve," Anna says, "you have had success. I mean, how many people knew you could sing a year ago, and how many people know it now?"

"But everything was supposed to be different!" says Eve. "We weren't just supposed to be sitting here watching TV and stuffing our faces like always."

"I wouldn't want a future where we weren't doing that," says Anna.

"Me neither," I agree.

Although, next year Anna will be spending more time with Nelson. And Eve will probably be busy with voice lessons and whatever new scheme she comes up with to get famous. And I'll be with Mark—I hope.

And who knows? Maybe next summer I will do that Julliard program. Or maybe I'll ask Liz if I can volunteer at her clinic. Either way, my mom's prediction will come true—the three of us won't be so "joined at the hip." But that's not scary to me anymore because I know we don't have to be to stay best friends.

Eve is silent a long time, so long that I think she's

fallen asleep. Then I hear, "Let's do another reading!"

I sputter, "Eve, after everything that's happened . . ."

She jumps up, switches on the light. "Let's do it for freshman year. Each does her own reading."

"And finds out what?" I demand.

"Whether freshman year of high school is going to suck, be great . . . stuff to look out for, stuff to look forward to." She turns to Anna. "Don't you want to find out what's going to happen to you and Nelson?"

Anna's quiet a moment. Then she says, "I'm not putting my future in the hands of fate anymore. From now on, I make my own decisions."

Frustrated, Eve turns to me. "Syd, don't you want to know what might happen for you and Mark?"

"No," I say firmly.

Eve pleads, "We know how to read them now. We wouldn't make the same mistakes."

"Yes, we would," I say. "And, anyway, the cards are at Anna's house."

Another silence. Then in a small voice Anna says, "Um, actually, they're not. I brought them with me."

"See!" Eve dives for Anna's bag. "I knew it."

"Anna . . ."

Apologetically, Anna says, "I thought it might be fun."

Fun, I think. *Fun to wonder about the future. Fun to worry. Fun to ask, Will I? Will he, will they? What if . . . ?*

Eve returns with the box. Sitting, she plunks it down between the three of us.

"Who wants to go first?"